The Birthday Killer

W. Kay Lynn

DEDICATION

This book is dedicated to God, my Creator and my inspiration. It is by His grace and love that I am where I am today.

ACKNOWLEDGMENTS

I would not have been able to complete this novel without the encouragement, advice and prayers of family and friends. I thank Patti, my sister, my rock, and greatest supporter for all the late night conversations and "writing retreats" to encourage me. I give thanks to Robin, my best friend, neighbor, and sidekick for being there to bounce ideas back and forth and keeping me grounded. Many thanks to Veeda, Annemarie and Jan for their reading and editing suggestions and their honest reactions. Thanks to Carol for her formatting assistance. And to Joyce, who never read anything I sent her, my thanks for taking me before our heavenly Father in prayer during this entire endeavor.

Chapter 1
Friday, February 18

The news of the peace agreement took top billing over everything. The early morning news program on the television kept repeating the good news, "The war is over! Our boys will be coming home!" The headlines in the morning newspaper read "PEACE HAS COME!" Even the story about the latest murder got only three inches of space in the lower left-hand corner of the front page. I suppose people needed something good to take their minds off the recent slayings that had rocked the local community. Lakin was a small, quiet town in East Texas where everyone knew everyone else. While the local Junior College brought a seasonal boost to the population and money to the businesses in town, there had never been any trouble associated with it. Speculation was running rampant; suggesting that some recently enrolled thug was responsible for the awfulness.

People just were not used to anything bad happening in Lakin. It was definitely the topic of conversation everywhere you went – the grocery store, the post office, the feed store and even at church. People started locking their doors when they were home and looking over their shoulders every time they went out. The peaceful atmosphere that normally permeated throughout the little town had been replaced with a sense of fear and suspicion.

In each of the past three months, a woman had been killed. According to the newspaper article, the police did not realize they had a problem until the third victim was found early yesterday morning. Each of the deceased had been teachers for the local school district, was single and had been murdered; two by strangulation and one by stabbing. So far, the Lakin Police Department had no positive leads as to whom the killer might be or why he chose his victims as he did. It was more than a little unnerving to realize that I, just like most of the teaching force in Lakin, could be targeted to be the next victim.

I glanced at the clock. It was only seven fifteen so I still had time for another cup of coffee before I had to leave for work. Molly, my four-month-old Terrier mix puppy, came bounding out of the bedroom where she had retrieved her blue tennis ball and dropped it at my feet. "So, you want to play a little ball before I leave, huh?" I smiled as I picked up the ball and rolled it across the kitchen floor. Her feet skidded in all directions on the tan and brown speckled linoleum flooring as she went scampering after it. I laughed as she pounced on the spherical object of her attention when it bumped to a stop against the cabinet on the far wall. She came strutting back carrying the ball in her mouth as though it was some grand trophy she had captured and dropped it at my feet. "One more time and then I'm going to have to head out," I told her as I stood up to put my breakfast dishes in the sink. I checked her food and water and set up the white plastic child safety gate in the entryway between the kitchen area and the living room. Since she was still in the chewing anything and everything stage, I wanted to make sure she didn't have an opportunity to demolish any unsuspecting object in my apartment.

"You be good today, girlfriend," I smiled as I reached down over the gate to rub Molly between the ears. I had found her at the animal shelter a few days after I moved into my apartment. I fell in love with her the moment I saw her. She had been in the pen with several other puppies, sitting in the corner with her back to the front of the enclosure. Her short white fur was interspersed with a few creamy beige and brown spots. One ear stood straight up while the other drooped like the flap on an envelope and I loved the way they were outlined with reddish brown hair along the front edges. When I called to her, she looked over her shoulder with the most terrified expression I had ever seen and my heart went out to her. As the shelter worker handed her to me, her eyes lit up and she started licking my chin. I knew we were destined to be best friends.

I surveyed the small one bedroom apartment as I completed a quick check to make sure all the lights were turned off. The gold shag carpet was worn and a bit outdated. The wood paneling on the walls was a few shades darker than I preferred but it was cozy and just perfect for my first place. Fortunately, I had been able to find the furnished apartment within walking distance from the school where I taught. I had graduated two weeks before Christmas and felt blessed to have found a teaching job in the middle of the year. They were definitely few and far between. During my interview with the Superintendent, George Nicholas, and the Director of Special

Education, Evelyn Gentry, I learned the reason for the opening. Mrs. Gentry explained that due to the large size of the special education class at West Elementary, the state education agency of Texas had allocated an additional teaching position. The current class had an enrollment of seventeen mentally handicapped students ranging in age from three to twenty-one. My class would consist of the eight youngest students in the group. I would officially start on January third when everyone returned from the Christmas holidays.

"That is, if you don't have plans to get married and move off as soon as you get here." Mr. Nicholas said with a wave of his hand.

"No, sir," I replied a little taken aback, "I hope to be here for a long time."

Mrs. Gentry smiled and winked, "Don't take him seriously; he is always saying things like that."

The two weeks before school started were full of constant, intense activity. I didn't even have time to celebrate Christmas. Not only did I have to find a place to live, move in and unpack; I also had to get my classroom set up and ready for my students. My days after Christmas were spent at the school arranging and rearranging desks, tables and shelves. Finally, I was satisfied that my classroom was comfortable and inviting. My evenings consisted of planning lessons and activities as well as making materials to use with the students. I wanted to make sure I was ready and everything would be perfect for the first day of my teaching career.

The cold air jolted me back to the present as I stepped out into the frigid winter air. "This is certainly a terrible time for my car to be in the shop!" I thought to myself as I tightened the scarf around my head to keep my hair from blowing and pulled my coat up around my neck. The crisp frosty air stung my eyes as it whipped around me and I knew the two-block walk to school would, out of necessity, be a fast one.

I could see the red brick building trimmed with white stone at the end of the street as soon as I stepped on the sidewalk in front of the apartments. The L-shaped, one story building was long across the front with window blinds drawn halfway up on all the windows of the classrooms facing the street. Two rooms already had lights on while the other five were still dark. A taller portion of the building at the left end housed the gym where the children were held until the bell rang at eight o'clock to mark the beginning of the school day. A driveway curved in front of the double doors by the gym and split with the left lane returning to the street and the right lane leading to a parking lot on the left side of the building. The whole block in front of the school building was lined with large, matured Red Oak trees spreading their branches over the center of the street.

W. Kay Lynn

Chapter 2
Friday, February 18

I was thankful for the warmth that welcomed me when I opened the heavy front door of the school. I waved a good morning to Amanda Post, the school secretary, as I passed the big plate glass windows that filled the front wall of the main office. I turned right at the first corner and headed to my room, the next to the last door on the left at the end of the long hall.

The first hour of activities were winding down when, just after nine o'clock, Mrs. Post opened my classroom door and stepped into the room. She was wearing a gray tweed pantsuit with a pale green sweater that complimented her hazel eyes. Her short cut silver-gray hair reminded me of my grandmother. I looked up from my desk where I had just sat down and smiled at her, "I was just getting ready to send in the lunch report. You really didn't have to come get it."

"You better hurry up with it or I'll have Mr. Brewer expel you for three days!" she teased. "No, really, Miss Carter, I came to watch your class. You have a visitor in the office and Mr. Brewer thought you would have more privacy there."

"No doubt about that!" I laughed as I surveyed the classroom. My students, ages three through eight, were all busy with various activities in the learning centers set up around the perimeter of the room. Tim and Randy were building roads and bridges with the wooden blocks. Donna, Tina, and Toni were cooking something special with the play dough in the home living area. Ronnie was dancing to a Hap Palmer record while Dave and Curtis were creating great works of art with the finger paint. "If I'm not back, we clean up at nine thirty and go sit on the rug for a story. The book for today is on the chalk tray. Just follow the schedule posted on the wall by the door. By the way, who is here? I wasn't expecting anyone."

"I'm not telling!" she smiled and raised her eyebrows. "You will just have to find out for yourself."

"OK! I'm gone. Be back as quick as I can." I promised as I pushed the door closed behind me.

I rounded the corner and went into the office. Allen Brewer, the Principal, was sitting at Mrs. Post's desk behind the four-foot high counter that divided the room into a small reception area and a slightly larger work area behind her desk. He was wearing a dark blue sweater vest over a light blue long sleeved shirt with a red and blue striped tie.

"Wow! I sure do like your new hair-do Mrs. Post." I laughed. "It's very becoming."

"You better be quiet. I'll have you arrested!" he replied, trying to look mean. Then with a more serious expression, he continued, "Go on in my office. They're waiting for you."

"THEY! Whew! I must be more popular than I realized," I laughed jokingly. As I entered Mr. Brewer's office I observed a man sitting behind the large maple desk, which was centered on the wall at the right end of the room in front of a matching credenza. On the wall above the credenza was an arrangement of Mr. Brewer's diplomas surrounded by various awards and honors he had received. Three matching Queen Anne armchairs covered with a colorful floral print were positioned in front of the desk. The wall opposite the door was lined with large windows draped with loosely woven blue linen curtains. The wall on the left end of the room was filled with a built-in maple bookcase, which hosted an assortment of books, framed photos and knick-knacks.

The tall, burly, slightly balding man who looked to be in his early forties stood up. His navy blue suit jacket opened slightly to reveal a handgun in the holster strapped to his side. He had the bluest eyes I had ever seen. He extended his hand across the desk and with a firm handshake said, "Miss Carter, I'm Detective Sam Reynolds." He quickly removed his hand from mine to cover a cough, excused himself and continued after a short pause. "You may know these two ladies; Mrs. Layne and Miss Martinez. Please sit down." He indicated the chair closest to the windows.

I knew Mrs. Layne, who was sitting in the chair nearest the door, but not very well. She was a member of the church I had been attending for the last six weeks since I moved to Lakin. Judy Layne, a petite woman with brown eyes and short black hair that softly framed her oval face, was a fifth grade teacher at South Elementary. Seated in the middle chair was Elizabeth Martinez, a tall and slender beauty with shoulder length curly auburn hair and dark brown eyes. While I had met her at a district wide teacher's meeting in early January, I didn't really know her. She taught sixth grade at North Elementary. I nodded and smiled at each of them and sat down.

Detective Reynolds was silent for a few minutes as he shuffled through some papers in the open folder lying on the desk in front of him. The other women and I exchanged puzzled glances. They were clearly as baffled as I about our meeting.

Detective Reynolds cleared his throat and looked up. "I guess you ladies are wondering what this is all about. I don't know if you read about it or not, but day before yesterday, another teacher was murdered. Her body was found yesterday morning.

"The reason for my meeting with you is to try to prevent one of you from being the next victim." He paused as Mrs. Layne let out a quiet gasp. "You may or may not be aware that each of the deceased teachers was killed on or near her birthday. All of you have birthdays next month. We have been up most of the night trying to gather as much information about these crimes as possible. We thought perhaps that the first two were merely coincidental in that they were both teachers, since the method of death was different. However, unfortunately too late, we regret that we did not take appropriate precautions before now. From what we can tell, it looks like we may have a serial killer on our hands," he informed us.

"What do we do?" How do we protect ourselves? Why haven't you caught them?" Miss Martinez nervously fired questions in rapid succession. "Are you sure one of us is next?"

"That's why I'm here, Miss Martinez," he replied in a patient, gentle voice. "Hopefully, we can all work together to figure out the answers to your concerns. I would like to go over the available details of each case with you. I realize this is extremely awkward and unpleasant and probably not exactly the way you planned to spend your Friday morning but I'm hoping that you may be able to add something to our investigation. Perhaps you can think of something that we have not considered or at the very least see things from a different angle and put a fresh perspective on the situation. Are there any other questions before we begin?"

The stunned expressions on our faces along with the heavy silence that had settled in the small room seemed to convey that we could not possibly think of anything more to ask at this moment. I found it difficult to breathe as I tried to wrap my mind around what he was actually saying.

Chapter 3
Friday, February 18

Alright then," he sighed deeply, "we'll start with the first one…Emily Watson. On the evening of Sunday, December nineteenth, the day after her twenty-seventh birthday, at six forty-two in the evening, Miss Watson's body was found by her fiancé, Ken Bridges.

When Mr. Bridges arrived at Miss Watson's apartment and knocked on the door, it opened slightly in response. It had been pulled closed but did not quite catch. He entered and found her lying on the living room floor. She had been strangled. Beside her body was an unsigned birthday card."

"Miss Watson, who lived alone, was supposed to go out that evening with her fiancé. He spoke to her briefly on the phone shortly after noon to let her know what time he would pick her up that evening and, according to Mr. Bridges, everything seemed to be fine. The coroner places her death between one thirty in the afternoon and six thirty in the evening. Mr. Bridges has been cleared as a suspect. There are several reputable witnesses who can verify his where abouts during that time frame. The neighbors reported nothing unusual. They did not see or hear anything that might be suspicious. Miss Watson had been teaching 6th grade for four years at South Elementary."

"It was a huge shock to all of us," Mrs. Layne said quietly. "She was such a sweet person and one of the best teachers I have ever known. Her students thought she hung the moon. They have really had a hard time adjusting to another teacher."

Detective Reynolds was quiet for a moment. "It's a shame that so many innocent people end up suffering because of the senseless act of one individual," he said in a kindly tone. With a reassuring nod toward us he continued, "On Tuesday evening, January eighteen, Jan Bowes returned home from choir practice at Lakin Baptist Church and found her roommate, Barbara Adams, on the floor of her bedroom. She had been stabbed numerous times. It was two days before her twenty-fourth birthday. This was her second year to teach Math at the High School. Again, the neighbors had nothing to report. It seems the two girls were very social and often had people visiting with them so no one paid any attention to who came or went anymore." He paused and made a visual check to see how we were receiving this information.

"We have no clear suspects. Miss Bowes states that Mrs. Adams had dated three different men in the past two years but they all checked out." He sighed heavily and shook his head.

"Wait! Are you saying *MRS*. Adams?" I interrupted. "I thought all the victims were single."

"Yes, I am saying Mrs. Adams. It seems that she got married right after high school graduation to her high school sweetheart. However, he turned out to be physically abusive and the union was not a good one. She was in the process of getting a divorce. We brought the estranged husband in for questioning but, so far, he has an unshakable alibi so we had to let him go. But he is definitely still a person of interest for the time being." The detective expounded.

"And then, yesterday morning, the seventeenth, we found Marie Hall," he continued. "She has been the Art teacher at Lakin Junior High for the past six years. She was twenty-eight. When she did not come to school or call in sick yesterday morning, the Principal called us to check it out. He really took it hard when we reported back to him. It seems that he had teased her the day before about watching out for the killer. They both had a real good laugh about it. The property owner let us in her apartment where we found her beside the dining room table. She too, had been strangled. An unsigned birthday card with a hand written message inside, identical to the first one, was on the table.

"In all three cases, while it was evident there had been a fierce struggle; the women definitely fought hard against their attacker, there were no signs of forcible entry. It is possible that the women knew the killer and willingly let him in."

"You said 'him'," commented Mrs. Layne. "Are you sure it's a man?"

"At this point, we aren't positive about anything except that we don't want it to happen again. We suspect a man from the bruises left on the victim's necks. It would take a mighty strong person to have made marks like that." He stated grimly.

"You found a card at the first and third victim's places but not at the second?" I asked for clarification.

"Actually there was one at the second murder. We just did not know about it until yesterday afternoon. The roommate, Miss Bowes, had picked it up off the living room floor when she entered the house. Apparently, Mrs.

Adams had gotten several birthday cards in the mail and put them on the mantle for display. Miss Bowes, thinking it had just fallen out of place, put the card on the mantle with the others. After the shock of finding her roommate's body and in all the activity associated with that, she did not think any more about it until we checked with her yesterday. It too matched the other cards and had the same handwritten message inside," he explained. "The presence of the card is one of several pieces of information that we haven't released to the public yet. I'd appreciate if you ladies wouldn't mention it to anyone."

"Were you able to get any fingerprints off any of the cards?" Mrs. Layne asked.

"Yes, we got a partial thumb print off the second card but it doesn't match anyone that we have in our files," he replied almost apologetically. "That's the only physical clue we have. None of the crime scenes had any unidentified fingerprints. We think the murderer wore gloves. There was no evidence of anything being wiped down."

"Any more questions?" he asked as he glanced at the papers in his folder again.

"Did they look alike? Did they look like … any of us?" Miss Martinez asked in a hushed voice.

"Not of any significance. One blond, two brunettes, two with brown eyes, one had green."

"Did they know any of the same people? Were there any other teachers with birthdays in those months?" I asked.

"I think y'all need to be on the police force. You have some good questions." He noted. "But seriously, as far as we know right now, outside of fellow teachers, we have no knowledge of them being associated with any of the same people. Of course, for that matter, we can't rule out the possibility that it isn't another teacher. As for your second question… yes." He shuffled through his papers and finding the one he wanted, continued, "In December there were three women teachers with birthdays – one on the second, one on the eleventh, and one on the eighteenth. In January there were six – one on the third, one on the seventh, one on the twelfth, two on the fourteenth, and one on the twentieth, and there were four this month – one on the second, one on the ninth, one on the twelfth, and one on the sixteenth. We do not know why he picked these particular women but we are working on that. We are not looking at the men teachers in the district at this time and are not including them in this data. Hopefully that is not a mistake."

We all exchanged nervous glances.

Chapter 4
Friday, February 18

I realize this is a difficult task for you but if we can get ahead of this guy, hopefully we will be able to stop him before this goes any further," Detective Reynolds said encouragingly as he looked from one person to the other. "Each of you will, of course, be under police surveillance while we are working on the case. We do not want to be obvious so we will use plain clothes police officers and undercover officers. We are bringing in extra officers from some of the surrounding counties to give us the manpower needed to ensure your safety. I met with Superintendent Nicholas earlier this morning to brief him of our plans. He assured me of the district's full cooperation during this whole ordeal."

"Do we need to hide out at home or maybe go out of town for the next month?" asked Mrs. Layne with a nervous laugh.

"No. We want you to go about your normal routine. Actually, Mrs. Layne, you are probably the least likely to be a victim since you are married. Two of the deceased were single while the third was in the process of becoming single. Mrs. Adams marital state did not appear to be common knowledge. That is not to say that you are in the clear. We just don't know at this time and we don't intend to take any unnecessary chances."

Detective Reynolds took a slow, deep breath. "Now," he said cautiously, "to the business at hand. Just start at the beginning and we will go from there. I want to know more about each of you. Where you came from. How long you have been here. Why you came here. Anything that might help to see if we can figure out who is most likely to be next." Detective Reynolds pulled a notepad out of his briefcase. "Mrs. Layne, why don't you go first? Tell me all about yourself."

"I hardly know where to begin," she paused briefly. "I was born on March twenty-fourth, at a very early age, near my mother."

"Uhhh...that's a good one but I don't think you have to go back quite that far," chuckled Detective Reynolds as we all had a good laugh.

"I'm sorry. I have wanted to use that line ever since I heard it several years ago at a church social. I just couldn't resist." You could feel the tension in the small office easing just a bit.

"OK," she continued, "I grew up in Wisconsin. By the time I graduated from high school, I decided I was tired of the cold, snow, and ice every winter. Therefore, I came to Texas to attend college. I have relatives in Huntsville and it was fairly easy for me to convince my parents to let me move there. I met my husband, Mark, during my senior year and we were married after I graduated from Sam Houston State College. We moved to Lakin eight years ago when Mark accepted the position as Editor of "The Lakin Daily Messenger".

"I must ask you to be discreet in your conversations with your husband about the things we are discussing today," Detective Reynolds interrupted. "I understand your need to talk with him about all of this but, as I said before, there are several facts about the murders that we are not revealing to the public at this time. I would not want any of this information to be compromised."

"Oh, I think it is safe to say that he won't print anything that doesn't come directly from your department. He is very sensitive to things of that nature," she answered.

"Good. Thanks. Please, go on." He replied with a nod.

"We have two children, Ashley is six and Mark Junior is three. I have been teaching at South Elementary since we moved here. I am a member of Lakin Community Church. I enjoy gardening and playing with my kids. My family is very important to me. What else do you want to know?"

"How old will you be on your birthday? Did you teach anywhere before you came to Lakin?" Detective Reynolds questioned.

"I will be thirty-four. I taught for two years in the Huntsville area while Mark finished working on his Master's degree. Then we moved here," she stated matter-of-factly.

"Why did you want to be a teacher?" Detective Reynolds asked.

"I just love children and I wanted to make a difference in their lives. I also enjoy learning new things along with them. It keeps me young," she replied with a chuckle as she fluttered her eyelashes.

Detective Reynolds studied his notes briefly. "I think that's all I need for now. Do either of you two ladies have any questions for Mrs. Layne?" he said as he looked up at us with raised eyebrows. "No? Who wants to be next?" he queried.

Miss Martinez spoke up. "I grew up in Rio Grand City in South Texas with two brothers and one sister. My Dad died when I was thirteen years old and Mom suddenly found herself the sole support for our family. With only a high school diploma and no special training, she had trouble finding adequate work that would pay enough to meet our needs. She strongly encouraged us to get a good education and have some training to fall back on in case we were ever in a similar situation." She paused for a moment and then added with a smile, "Mom thought girls should be either a nurse or a teacher. I volunteered as a Blue Bird at our local hospital during my early high school years but that just was not for me. I'm glad I chose teaching. I really enjoy it."

"How long have you been teaching? When is your birthday and how old will you be?" queried Detective Reynolds, pen poised over his notepad.

"I have been teaching third grade at North Elementary since I graduated from Pan American College in Edinburg five years ago. I will be twenty-seven on March ninth," she stated straightforwardly.

"That's Edinburg, Texas, right? Or are you a world traveler?" Detective Reynolds smiled.

She replied with a smile, "Yes, it's Texas."

"Okay, ladies. Any questions for her?" he paused.

"Thanks Miss Martinez. Miss Carter, why don't you go ahead and give us your background information," Detective Reynolds directed.

"Sure," I replied. "My birthday is March fifteenth and I will be thirty-two years old. I grew up in East Texas just outside of Nacogdoches. I graduated from Stephen F. Austin State University this past December and started teaching here in January."

"What took you so long?" asked Detective Reynolds. "Oh, I'm sorry. That sounded rude and that is really not the way I meant it." He added sheepishly.

"No offense taken." I chuckled. "I was late completing college because I stayed home to take care of my ailing parents. Mother was ill for quite some time before she died in February, two years ago. Dad only lasted about another six months after her death. I was able to take a few classes here and there through the years but I wasn't able to go full time until last year after Dad passed away."

"Why did you want to be a teacher?" asked the Detective.

"And why did you go into Special Education? Isn't that hard?" added Mrs. Layne.

"Well, I have always wanted to teach. When I was a little girl, we would play school in the summer time. I would get my little sister and her friends and we would have 'school' in the garage. We used boxes for desks and we had a small chalkboard. I taught them to read, basic counting and even some simple addition. I'm sure their first grade teachers hated me!" I chuckled at the memory.

"As for Special Education, no, I don't think it is any harder. I was working at a summer camp several years ago and the program had a week of camp for mentally retarded children. I was a little nervous at first, but as I worked with them, I realized that they were really not any different than other children. They just have a different way of learning. After a few days, it was sort of like the sun came up and it dawned on me …I knew God's plan for my life included teaching children with special needs. So far, I love it!"

"Hmm, that's interesting," Detective Reynolds remarked thoughtfully. "Any more questions for her?" He paused momentarily. "Do you have any for me?" he added, his eyebrows rose in anticipation. "If not, I guess that about does it. Let me give you my card. If you have *any* questions, please feel free to call me. Try to have an enjoyable weekend and don't worry. We have some time to get this matter taken care of and I will be meeting with you again to keep you informed about our progress. I will be keeping my eye on you!" he assured us as he handed each of us a business card. "We are here for your protection and we take that job very seriously. And, by the way, if you happen to notice any of the undercover men assigned to watch you, they should give you a signal to let you know who they are. They will touch their right ear with their left hand," he demonstrated. "Good day, ladies. I will be in touch." He stood and opened the office door. We filed out in silence.

Chapter 5
Friday, February 18

As I walked out of the office, I checked my watch. I was surprised that it was only eleven forty. The past two and a half hours seemed like a month. The walk back to my room took twice as long as usual. My whole body was numb. I felt like I was walking in a fog. There was so much rumbling around in my brain that I couldn't sort it all out. My mind was so overwhelmed that even in the shadow of danger I really didn't feel threatened; like we had just spent the last two and a half hours talking about somebody else...not me and the other two women. However, the thought of Detective Reynolds "keeping an eye" on me brought a strange sense of comfort.

As I opened the door to my classroom I was met by a line of students. "We were just lining up to go to lunch," Mrs. Post informed me. "You look terrible! Are you alright?" she added as the students swarmed about me with squeals of welcoming glee.

"I'll be fine," I responded above the bobbing heads surrounding me. "I hope I'm just having a bad dream. Pinch me." I held out my arm, "See if I wake up!"

Mrs. Post patted my hand and smiled above the din, "If there is anything I can do to help, please let me know."

"Thanks, I appreciate that. Apparently, the next few weeks are going to be really stressful! Thanks for staying with my kids. Sorry it took so long. I hope they didn't give you too much trouble." I sighed apologetically.

"They were fine, really. They kept asking where you were. When I told them you were in the office, Tim wanted to know if you said a bad word and had to go to time-out.," she laughed.

"I think that happens quite often at home," I shook my head. "OK guys; let's get back in line so we can go to lunch." I turned my attention on the wriggling bodies encircling me.

The Birthday Killer

"See you later. Enjoy the rest of your day," Mrs. Post encouraged as she closed the door behind her.

I was thankful for the squirming group in front of me. I would not have time to think about the events to come while I was with them. They would definitely command every moment of my attention while we were together.

The remainder of the day was a blur of activities. I went through the motions of our well-established procedures as if on autopilot.

On the short walk home, I was acutely aware of everything around me; the wind whistling shrilly through bare tree branches, squirrels scampering across the dry ground through rustling leaves in search of their hidden treasures, and people bundled up against the frigid air walking hurriedly to their own destinations. As the reality of this morning's discussion began to sink in, I was terrified to think what the next few weeks would hold. As usual, Molly was excited to see me when I got home. She jumped, yelped, and ran around in circles as I crossed the living room to free her from the kitchen.

"Hey, did you miss me, girlfriend?" I laughed nervously. "Just wait until you hear about my day! You won't believe what's going on!" I caught her as she jumped into my arms. "Let's go outside so you can take care of business," I suggested as I hooked her leash, grabbed her ball, and headed out the door.

My imagination went into overdrive. I glanced furtively at every bush and tree; scouring the landscape as we walked the length of the landing in front of the second floor apartments, down the stairs, around the end of the building and through the gate to the empty lot behind the small apartment complex. She took off like a shot when I released her from her leash. She raced in and out of the Redbud trees that lined the outer edges of the lot just inside the fence. Their tiny buds were maturing and would soon be bursting forth with a beautiful splash of color in the otherwise drab landscape. Each corner of the lot hosted a cluster of Azalea bushes arching around a cement bench.

After about ten minutes of playing fetch with the ball, we were both ready to go back in where it was warm and cozy. As I rounded the corner to the front of the building, I noticed a man across the street sitting in his car. He watched as we walked to the stairs. He gave no signal. I tried not to look at him but my eyes were repeatedly drawn to this potential threat. I looked for the undercover man but could not see him anywhere. A wave of fear like I nothing I had ever known before washed over me. I hurried Molly up the stairs and in to the apartment.

Once inside I scooped her up and hugged her close. "Oh Molly, I wish you were a great big dog instead of just a little puppy," I breathed anxiously. "Do you think I should call the police? I don't want to let my imagination run away with me. They would probably just laugh at me for over reacting at every little thing." I decided not to call since I was inside and safe. I had trouble falling asleep; listening to every creak and pop as the old building reacted to the falling nighttime temperatures. The sounds that I had grown accustomed to became ominous predictors of impending doom.

Chapter 6
Monday, February 21

Monday morning dawned bright and clear. There was not a cloud in the sky and the blustery wind of the past few days had settled to an occasional frigid puff. The weekend had been rather uneventful; just the usual housekeeping chores on Saturday morning and church on Sunday. I really just wanted to lock myself away in my apartment but Detective Reynolds had said we needed to try to behave normally. I didn't feel normal; I was not even sure what that was. I looked for the undercover man every time I had taken Molly outside, when I went to the grocery store for a few items and even on my way to church. However, I never saw him. I could only hope and pray he was doing his job.

I talked with Mrs. Layne at church. She had not spotted her undercover man either. She figured that was just the way it was supposed to be. After all, if *we* were able to spot them then the killer would too and the police might not be able to catch him. While her reasoning was sound, the idea offered very little reassurance.

After securing Molly in the kitchen, I headed out to school. It was nippy but at least it wasn't too bad since the wind had stopped blowing. I walked rapidly while trying to be nonchalant in searching my surroundings for anyone suspicious. I was probably a lot more conspicuous than I would be if I were behaving "normally". Everyone I passed seemed intent on reaching his or her own destinations as quickly as possible with no thought of me. I breathed a sigh of relief when I arrived at school. My classroom was warm and inviting. It gave me a comforting sense of security…I felt safe there.

Monday and Tuesday came and went like any ordinary day. Routine activities helped to pass the time and keep a sense of normalcy to life. The uncertainty of the future was always at the back of my mind but the engaging structure of my classroom was reassuring. Last Friday was starting to feel like a figment of my imagination. On Wednesday afternoon, during rest time, there was a tap on my classroom door. I opened it to find Detective

Reynolds standing there. He was wearing a dark brown suit with a tan shirt and brown and red paisley tie. The bulge at his waistline gave evidence to the gun he wore. "Come on in," I invited quietly. "Do you have any news?" I inquired.

"Not really. I just wanted to check in with you and get an idea of your classroom setup so if we needed to put a man in here with you we could do it with the least amount of disruption," he replied.

"Do you think it will come to that? Do you think we are in danger at school?" I asked alarmed; a surge of panic coursed through my body.

"No, not at all. We're just trying to cover all possible scenarios," he smiled encouragingly. "Why does your class look so different from Mrs. Layne's and Miss Martinez's classes?" he inquired as he gazed around the room with a puzzled expression on his face.

"Their classes are for older students. Young children and students with disabilities like mine learn best when they can manipulate things and become involved in doing something with them," I explained. "So, my class is set up in centers or specific areas where the children can do fun activities to learn different skills. Let me give you the guided tour." We started at the door and moved to the right to each area in the room "As you can see, each of the different areas are separated by low bookshelves. The bookshelves hold the current learning materials for that particular center. This first space is the 'Blocks' area and this week we are learning about 'long' and 'short'. They can use the square blocks and the rectangular blocks to build anything they can imagine – houses, a fort, and streets – you name it – they build it. The next area is the 'Home Living' area. Here we have a child sized stove with little pots and pans, refrigerator, sink, table and chairs, ironing board and a stand-up mirror. They can cook, wash dishes, feed the baby doll, etc. The blue chest against the wall has different kinds of clothes, shoes, hats and purses so that they can play dress up."

I glanced at Detective Reynolds as we reached the end of the first wall. "Are you with me?" I asked.

"I think so," he answered hesitantly. "Keep going."

"OK. Next we have the 'Listening / Music' area," I said as we turned to focus on the back wall of the classroom. "Here they can play a record on the record player, listen to a tape on the tape recorder or play one of the instruments that are available and create their own tunes. Next is the 'Library' area. They can sit in the rocker or get comfortable on the cushions on the floor and read the books on display. They can also take one of the books on tape and …"

"They can read?" he interrupted; looking surprised and sounding amazed.

"Well, they 'read' the pictures. But some of the older kids can follow along in the book while they are listening to someone read it on the tape recorder," I explained.

He nodded thoughtfully while giving an understanding smile. "OK."

"Moving on, we have the 'Manipulatives' area. Here they can put puzzles together, string beads, sew or lace holes in cardboard shapes, copy patterns or make designs with the peg boards," I continued, indicating the centers by the windows. "In the 'Art' area we use crayons, chalk, markers, finger paint, watercolors, tempera paint, and even shaving cream. They usually have two or three choices every day. The small table between the windows and my desk is our 'Nature' area. That can include pretty much anything…leaves, rocks, and sticks…things we find outside.

"Across the front of the room is my desk and the kidney shaped table. The table is where I pull one or two kids at a time to focus on something they need to be learning; like writing their name, cutting with the scissors, different math activities, and whatever else is appropriate. And last, but not least, is the big rug in the center of the room. That is where we do large or whole group activities with all the kids sitting down together. We talk about the calendar – days of the week, months of the year; the weather – what kind of clothes we should wear; the different numbers, letters, colors, shapes, and everything we are studying for the week. I try to make the activities in the centers match what we are learning that week. Can you guess what our focus is for this week?" I asked him with a smile.

"I'm tired just listening to you," he answered with a quiet chuckle. "Let me see. I would guess orange has something to do with it. I notice a lot of orange colored stuff around."

"Yep, you got it. Orange is our color this week so I try to have it everywhere," I confirmed. "We are also learning the letters 'K' and 'L', the number six, long and short, and stars," I added. "That's why we have orange dishes and play dough with star cookie cutters in the Home Living area, orange finger paint and crayons in the Art area, long and short blocks and orange cars in the Block area and so on."

"OK. I think I understand," he said uncertainly. "Thanks for the tour."

It felt comfortable with him in the room. He had an easy-going manner about him that was very appealing and a sense of competence that was reassuring.

"Last Friday afternoon I saw a man watching me from his car across the street from my apartment," I remarked timidly. "I tried to locate the undercover man but I couldn't see him anywhere. Are you sure he's there?" I questioned. "I started to call but I didn't want you to think I was over reacting." I added.

"The man in the car was Robert Binder. He was waiting for his ex-wife to get home with their daughter so he could pick her up for his monthly visitation. Your guy *is* on the job. You might not see him but he's there," he smiled reassuringly. "Did you have any other questions for me?" he added, giving me a genuine look of interest.

"Several, actually," I replied with a nervous chuckle, "but I'm not sure you have enough time to answer them all."

"Why don't you make a list and we will go over them first thing Friday morning," he suggested. "I'll have the other teachers come over so we can meet again. I know they probably have questions, too"

"OK, I will. I'm sorry I'm so nervous about this," I whispered.

"You have no reason to apologize. I would be worried if you *weren't* somewhat apprehensive. This is a very serious situation but I want you to know that we are doing everything in our power to keep you safe," he assured me with a warm smile.

"Thank you," I smiled shyly. "That means a lot."

"I will see you Friday morning," he confirmed as he turned to leave. "And if you have *any* other suspicious situations, please, call me. You have my card. I don't want you to be afraid when it isn't necessary," he added seriously.

"OK," I nodded. "Thank you." He closed the door softly behind him. I was sorry to see him go.

Chapter 7
Friday, February 25

The sun had just started peeking up over the horizon when my eyes popped open. My heart was beating rapidly. What was it? Did a noise wake me up? I looked down bedside the bed at Molly who was still sleeping soundly on her blanket. No, it couldn't have been or she would have alerted to it. Then I remembered. It was Friday and today was the day that Detective Reynolds would be coming to school. Why did my heart flutter when I thought of that?

I lay there as the room began to lighten with the dawn and let my mind wander to the first time I had seen him. His sturdy frame was just less than six feet tall. His square jaw and wide cheekbones fit well on his broad shoulders. When we shook hands, even though his hands were soft, I could feel his strength. I also noticed he didn't have on a wedding band. And his beautiful eyes...the alarm shattered the quiet and brought me back to the present. I laughed as Molly sprang to life and started jumping up and down.

"Hang on girl. Let me get some clothes on and I'll take you outside," I said as I reached for the off button on the clock and turned the covers back with one continuous motion. I dreaded these times of taking her out. I was on constant alert; afraid that someone was going to jump out and grab me. I just couldn't get used to the idea that someone was there; some hidden protector was watching out for my safety.

I was glad Molly did not linger on these nippy mornings but took care of business promptly. We were back in the apartment in a matter of minutes. We went to the kitchen where I gave her some fresh water and food.

"You better watch me, Molly," I said as I started cooking eggs and toast for breakfast. "I feel like a giddy school girl this morning. All because I am going to see a man I do not really know! I'm just sorry I had to meet him under such scary conditions." Molly looked at me with her head cocked to one side. "I know. You are right. I am just a job to him. I think all this crazy stuff going on has my head all mixed up! But he does seem nice." I smiled as I reached down to rub her head. "Hey, go get your ball and I'll play with you while I eat." I encouraged her. She went scurrying to find it while I sat down at the dining table and started eating.

I had gotten my car back Wednesday afternoon but it was such a pretty morning I decided to walk to school anyway. My eyes continually scanned the areas around me as I walked. The air was crisp and invigorating; it was going to be a beautiful day! I was a little surprised by how keenly I was looking forward to the meeting with Detective Reynolds. My anticipation level was rising with every step closer I got to school.

The morning seemed to drag on forever. I wondered why it was taking so long for everyone to get here for the meeting. The detective had said he would be here first thing in the morning. I kept watching the door; knowing that at any moment Mrs. Post would be coming to watch my class while I went to meet with Detective Reynolds and the other teachers.

Finally, after lunch when I had just finished putting the children down on their mats and turned on some soft music for rest time, Mrs. Post slipped quietly in the door. "They're all here now. I'll watch the little ones while you're gone," she whispered. "You may come back and find me napping with them," she added with a smile.

"That would be fine," I teased. "There is an extra mat in that cabinet. They sleep for about an hour and then get up for a snack. We have orange Kool-Aid and lion shaped cookies today," I indicated the cooler by my desk.

Detective Reynolds looked up from his seat behind the desk and nodded solemnly when I opened the office door. There was a heavy silence in the small room. Mrs. Layne, sitting in the first chair, looked very tense and Miss Martinez, who was sitting in the middle chair, was visibly shaken; her face pale and eyes red from crying.

"What happened?" I exclaimed as I sat down in the chair nearest the windows.

"Miss Martinez received a note from the killer this morning," Detective Reynolds stated quietly as Miss Martinez stifled a sob.

"What!" I exclaimed. "Are you sure it was from the killer? How do you know?" I reached over and put my hand on her shoulder as I addressed Detective Reynolds.

"Yes, we're sure. It contained some of the same verbiage that the cards left at the murder scenes had in them," he replied somberly.

"What did it say?" I inquired.

He handed me a Polaroid picture of a yellow piece of paper that had a message scrawled in large, green, block letters.

"YOUR BIRTHDATE WILL BE HERE SOON. I WILL HELP YOU CELEBRATE."

"How did he get it to you?" I laid the picture on the edge of the desk and turned back to Miss Martinez.

"It was taped to the outside of my windows at school," she choked. "He knows which room is mine! I can't go back there!" Her voice rose as she squeaked out her fears.

"Isn't this out of character? I mean, he didn't go to any of the other classrooms did he?" Mrs. Layne asked sternly; her voice full of apprehension.

"Well," said Detective Reynolds slowly. "Not that we can determine in the first two cases but possibly in the third one."

"What do you mean?" I demanded with furrowed brows.

"While we were interviewing the staff on each campus no one mentioned hearing Miss Watson or Mrs. Adams say anything about any kind of note or anything suspicious. However, it appears that about two weeks before her death Miss Hall told another teacher about a note she found taped to her classroom window. She thought it was from a student because the writer had misspelled 'birthday' and wrote 'birthdate' instead. Apparently, she threw it away. We don't know exactly what it said but it would be fairly probable that it had been from the killer."

"How does the note Miss Martinez got compare to the message in the birthday cards?" I asked. "Why didn't you tell us about the note on Miss Hall's window?"

Detective Reynolds let out a long sigh. "It's similar. The cards were written in the same style and said 'What a way to celebrate your last birthdate. Glad I could help.' The cards were the kind that had a picture on the front, in this case it was purple Irises, and were blank on the inside. They were probably purchased from the dime store last spring; that was when they first came out. They were sold in packages of six and the store had a dozen packages. There is no way of finding out who purchased them or how many packages they purchased because the store does not keep that kind of records. I didn't say anything because I thought it was just something different he did in Miss Hall's situation. We don't know if it happened with the first two women or not."

The room was quiet for several minutes. The air was thick with apprehension. Finally Detective Reynolds spoke, "If there are no other questions, you ladies are free to go back to your classes. Miss Martinez, I understand your principal has released you for the day and you can go home.

We will have extra men covering you. I know that's not much comfort but it's our only option right now. And we will have an officer at your school, full time, starting next week," he added.

We all stood to leave. "Miss Carter, may I speak to you for just a minute?" I looked at Detective Reynolds standing behind the desk.

"Sure," I said as I sat back down.

When the door closed, he came around the desk, turned the middle chair to face me and sat down. "This may not be the most appropriate time but I…Um, I was wondering if you had any plans for this evening," he said hastily. "If not, I would like to invite you out to eat."

"Oh," I whispered in astonishment. "No, I don't have anything planned for tonight. It would be nice to go out to eat. Thanks."

"Good. Then I'll pick you up about seven?"

"OK. See you then," I stood and walked to the door. "I guess you know where I live," I turned to look at him.

He smiled and nodded.

Chapter 8
Friday, February 25

I haven't been on a date since my sophomore year in college," I exclaimed to Molly who was sitting in the middle of my bed wagging her tail as fast as it would go. After Mom became ill and needed constant care, I had dropped out of school to take care of her. My social life, which was almost nonexistent to begin with, had also been put on hold; there was no time to spend with friends.

"Hey girl, what do you think of this outfit?" I held up a pair of black linen slacks and a light green, long sleeve, mohair sweater with green pearl buttons up the front. "Or do you like this better?" I asked indicating a pair of dark brown corduroy pants and a bulky, multi-hued blue knit pullover. Molly cocked her head to one side and then the other as she studied me from the bed. She gave a playful bark and rolled over on her back. Then quick as a wink she sat back up and barked again. "Why, you're absolutely right! The brown pants will definitely be warmer and the mohair sweater will add just the right touch of dressy. You sure know fashion, girlfriend." I scratched behind her ears and she melted in pure delight.

I stood in front of the bathroom mirror for the umpteenth time checking my appearance. I was satisfied with the reflection. The gray-green eyes sparkled with excitement. The naturally rosy, high cheekbones and slightly rounded face were framed by shoulder length, wavy, medium brown hair pulled back on the sides and secured with light green combs that matched my sweater. I wasn't sure if my jitters were the result of the stressful situation I had been thrown into or just the anticipation of an evening with the detective. Probably a little of both, I figured.

I jumped when the doorbell rang and Molly barked. I checked the clock on the bathroom wall. "He's certainly punctual! Seven o'clock sharp!" I whispered as I crossed the living room to open the door. He stood there smiling holding a single red rose. My heart skipped a beat.

W. Kay Lynn

"Wow! You look great!" he exclaimed as he held out the rose. "This is for you."

"Thank you," I laughed shyly as I lifted the rose to sniff the delicate fragrance. "Come on in. I'll just put this in a glass of water." I turned toward the kitchen as Detective Reynolds closed the door. Molly spun around in a circle and sat down in front of him with her tail wagging so fast it shook her whole body. "That's Molly," I introduced. "Apparently she really likes you."

"That's me," he quipped, "adored by little old grandmothers and cute little puppies. Hey girl." He stooped down to pet her.

I set up the gate and Detective Reynolds picked her up and set her over the barrier onto the kitchen floor. "I guess she is in solitary confinement while you are gone?" he smiled.

I chuckled and nodded affirmatively. "Yes, bless her heart. She gets to spend too much time in here but she doesn't seem to mind."

"I'm ready to go, if you are," he motioned toward the door.

"I'm good to go. Where are we going?" I asked.

"How do you feel about Mexican Food?"

"That sounds great. It's not something I cook at home very often."

Detective Reynolds locked the door and pulled it closed behind us.

Chapter 9
Friday, February 25

The Green Sombrero was hopping with activity. The orange, square, stucco building with hot pink borders painted around the door and windows was topped with, not surprisingly, a giant, grass green sombrero. The parking lot was almost full; apparently, it was the Friday night place to be. We were directed to a bench on the front wall for a twenty-minute wait before being seated.

"I heard about this place but I haven't had a chance to try it out. They certainly live up to their name," I observed. Each booth that lined the outer walls had a lighted, green sombrero lamp hanging over it. The tables that filled the inner part of the room were each adorned with small green ceramic sombreros with a red candle sticking out of the middle of the top.

"The décor is rather corny but the food is good," Detective Reynolds offered. "How do you like living in Lakin?" he asked.

"Well, Detective Reynolds, until a week ago I thought it was a really nice place to be."

"Hold on…just a minute. The detective got off work at five thirty. In addition, this isn't a business date. Please, call me Sam."

"OK," I smiled. "How long have you been in Lakin? Did you grow up here or what?"

"Um, that would be what. I was raised in Waco. Spent a couple of years after high school being a bum until my parents gave me an ultimatum. Went to the Police Academy at the Junior College and came here when I graduated from the program."

"Why Lakin?"

"Followed a girl. Didn't work out. She moved on to greener pastures. I liked it here so I stayed." He answered in a straightforward manner.

"How long have you been here?" I continued to probe.

"Seventeen years. Started out as a Patrolman and worked my way up to Detective. Lakin is a good town. The people are friendly. Fairly peaceful. At least until you moved here." His eyes twinkled as he teased me.

27

"Oh, so now I'm the prime suspect?"

"Hardly," he chuckled. "But I aim to keep you under close supervision, just to be sure." He winked and his blue eyes laughed.

The hostess indicated that our table was ready and led the way past several empty tables to a circular booth in the far corner of the dining room. "Thanks, Mandy," Sam said to the teenaged girl who placed menus in front of us after we were seated.

"Hey, Detective Reynolds, have you, uh...caught that man who is killing those women?" Mandy said with a slight tremor in her voice.

"No, Mandy. Not yet but we are working on it. We'll get him," he reassured her.

"I hope it doesn't take too long," she responded. Then switching back to her business role, "Bobbi Sue will be your server. Sorry it took so long for your booth to be ready. Enjoy your meal," she smiled as she turned to go.

"*Your* booth?" I raised an eyebrow.

Well," he confessed sheepishly, "They know I like to sit with my back to the wall. I want to be able to see what is happening around me."

"So you come here often?" I surmised.

"I guess you could call me a regular. Is there anything in particular you like? I usually get the fajitas. They do them up right! I would definitely recommend them."

"That sounds good. And I just want water to drink."

Bobbi Sue brought a large green sombrero shaped bowl with chips around the outer edge and "the best homemade salsa ever", according to Sam, in the center. She took our order, grinning the whole time. Based on the looks we were getting I got the distinct impression that I was under scrutiny of the locals.

"Am I just being paranoid or does everybody keep looking at us?" I asked.

"No. They're looking. You're new in town. Moreover, uh, I don't usually have an attractive woman dining with me. Normally it's just me and some of the guys from the force."

The dish of sizzling, smoky fajitas arrived, preceded by their delicious aroma. Sam bowed his head and said a quick prayer of blessing for our food. The tender pieces of well-seasoned meat were just as extraordinary as promised. There was a slight lull in conversation as we began eating but it didn't last long. "Do you go to church?" I asked.

"Most of the time," he replied. "I usually go to the Methodist Church on Spring Street. I know where you go. Do you like it?"

"Yes, I really do. I feel at home there…like I belong. I did not bother visiting any other churches. I just knew I was in the right place."

"What about your family?" he inquired. "What are they like?"

"My parents taught us the importance of God and family. We always did things together. We went to church, played games, visited aunts and uncles, and grandparents. Family togetherness was an important ingredient in our everyday lives. We were taught to respect others, always play fair and honor God in all we did. My sister and her husband are living in our parents' house since they died. My brother followed his wife to Vermont so I don't see him as often anymore. That about sums it up. What about you?"

"Not much different. We had a lot of family time, too. I have an older brother who still lives in Waco not far from our parents. I visit with them every couple of months. What keeps you busy when you aren't teaching?"

"I love to read, play games, puzzles, work on things for school. Just stuff." I shrugged. "Oh, and of course, play with Molly," I added.

"What kind of puzzles do you do?"

"All different kinds – jigsaw puzzles, word puzzles, brain teasers. I just like to figure things out. I enjoy the challenge. Actually, I would love to see all the information you have on the murders, if possible. There has to be some clue, some pattern to how he is thinking. Is there any way I could do that?"

"That can be arranged. What are you doing Sunday afternoon?" He asked.

"Nothing, at the moment. Why don't you come over for lunch?" I invited. "I don't want to see any pictures. Just the facts," I added hurriedly.

Sam laughed. "It's a date. I will bring over what we have and we can look at it. Maybe you can find something we are missing. And the looks I keep getting from Mandy say it's time for us to be leaving. I think it is closing time."

"Already? I didn't realize we had been here that long!" I exclaimed in surprise. I hadn't even noticed when Bobbi Sue cleared the dishes off the table.

Sam checked the apartment and insisted on going with me to walk Molly. Only after I dead-bolted the door and latched the safety chain did I hear him walking away. It was a nice feeling to know he was concerned for me.

Chapter 10
Sunday, February 27

I hummed as I prepared a roast with onions, potatoes and carrots and put them in the oven. They would be ready when I got home from church. Then as soon as Sam got here, we could eat. After getting Molly settled, I headed out to church.

During the second stanza of the third hymn, Sam slid into the pew beside me. "Sorry to be late. I got stuck at the office when I stopped to get the files," he whispered. We shared the hymnal. I had not been expecting him to come to my church and I certainly was not expecting the rich baritone that joined me on the chorus. I had trouble concentrating on the sermon with him sitting so close to me. Nevertheless, I had to admit it was really nice to feel the strength of his presence.

Sam took Molly downstairs while I got lunch on the table. "I can smell that clear down to the bottom of the stairs," he informed me as he unhooked Molly's chain when they came back in. "I can't wait to taste it."

After lunch, Sam helped clear the table and spread out the files he had brought from the office. We decided to have dessert after we went through all the reports and information. I drew out a calendar of the last three months on a piece of poster board; leaving room at the bottom for notes.

"OK," he sighed. "Here is what we know."

I made notes on the poster board as he read a copy of the police report for each crime.

Victim #1: Emily Watson –
    blond, brown eyes, 5'2", 106 pounds
    Engaged
    DOB: December 18
    Died: December 19
    Age: 27
    Taught: South Elementary – 6th Grade– 5th year in Lakin

Lived alone, second floor apartment, Bishop Street
Found in living room – strangled – card next to body

Victim #2: Barbara Adams –
    brunette, green eyes, 5'5", 128 pounds
    Married to high school sweetheart; legally separated
        – Divorce pending – spousal abuse
    DOB: January 20
    Died: January 18
    Age: 23
    Taught: High School Math – 2nd year in Lakin
    Lived in house with roommate - Baxley Road
    Found in bedroom – stabbed - card in living room

Victim #3: Marie Hall –
    brunette, brown eyes, 5'4", 123 pounds
    No current boyfriend
    DOB: February 16
    Died: February 16
    Age: 28
    Taught: Junior High Art – 7th year in Lakin
    Lived alone, first floor apartment, Maple Tree Street
    Found in dining room – strangled - card on table

"I made copies of the photos and cards from each crime scene," Sam stated. "I did not include any pictures of the bodies," he added quickly when I winced at the mention of crime scene photographs.

"Thanks," I smiled appreciatively. "I know there has to be something here to help us figure out what's going on. I just wish I knew what it is we are looking for."

I laid the black and white pictures out on the poster board next to their corresponding victim. They all showed evidence of the struggles that had taken place. Furniture was shoved out of place, chairs and small tables were turned over. I shuddered at the thought of what the women must have gone through. The copies of the cards showed the same crude message scrawled in all capital letters on each. **"WHAT A WAY TO CELEBRATE YOUR LAST BIRTHDATE. GLAD I COULD HELP."** Other than the spacing between the words, the cards were identical.

I studied the notes, comparing similarities and differences between the victims, checking the dates and intervals, and tried to fit the three of us who were possible targets into the mix.

"Age wise, Miss Martinez figures to be the prime target. She is the only one of us in her twenties. Mrs. Layne and I are too old." I reflected.

"There are thirty days between the first and second murders. There are twenty-nine days between the second and third murders. There are twenty-eight days between the third murder and my birthday," I observed. "And Mrs. Layne's birthday is the last one in the month like all the victims. But that doesn't fit with your theory that he is only targeting single women unless he knew Mrs. Adams was married."

"And that would blow that theory," Sam noted.

"That didn't help narrow it down any, did it?" I surmised. "There has to be something else. What am I missing?" I studied the poster.

"It's not just you who is missing it. We are all perplexed by this. There doesn't seem to be any solid theory to figuring it out." Sam consoled. "Certainly nothing obvious!" I continued to look at the poster of information, pondering over every detail.

"Is it too late for that peach cobbler you were teasing me with earlier?" he asked after a slight pause in conversation.

"Absolutely not! Do you want ice cream on it?" I replied, glad for a diversion from our present activity.

"Well, yeah!" he responded with pretend astonishment. "Is there any other way to eat it?" The afternoon passed too quickly before Sam took his leave.

"Oh, Molly," I sighed as I got ready for bed later that evening. "I don't know if I like it here anymore. Seeing all the evidence and notes makes it too real. The apartment seems so empty and frightening with Sam gone. My feeling of security walked out the door when he left. This is *not* fun."

Chapter 11
Monday, February 28

During the morning announcements, Mr. Brewer informed us that there would be a brief Faculty Meeting at the end of the school day that everyone must attend. After the last bell and all students had gone, we made our way one-by-one to the meeting. Superintendent Nicholas, flanked by Mr. Brewer and Detective Reynolds, addressed the group of educators and school staff assembled in the school library.

"These are troublesome times," he began. "I know each one of you, as well as everyone else in the district, is acutely aware of the events of the last three months. I am here to assure you that we, the administration of Lakin ISD, are working closely with the Police Department to ensure that your well-being is guaranteed to the best extent possible. Detective Reynolds and I," he indicated Sam and himself, "are meeting with each campus to let all of you know what security measures we are putting in place and hopefully that will give you some peace of mind. The safety of our staff and students is of the utmost priority. Detective," he nodded at Sam and with a wave of his hand indicated that Sam should step up to speak.

"Thank you Mr. Nicholas," Sam nodded. "First, let me say that the department appreciates your willingness to cooperate with us. It makes our job easier knowing we have your full support in this matter." Turning to face the group, he continued, "We will be doubling our patrols around the schools during the day, as well as, more frequent overnight patrols in the neighborhoods. We are also adding extra phone lines and personnel in the dispatcher's office. We will have extra officers on duty around the clock, as well. If you notice anyone or anything suspicious, here at school or around your neighborhood, call us. We will send an officer to check it out."

Amid the murmuring voices, someone from the back of the room spoke out. "Are you saying something might happen at school?"

"No," Sam answered. "We don't think there is any real danger at school. We are just being cautious and trying to be proactive. We want to be ready for any and all possible developments."

"If there are no other questions," Mr. Nicholas stepped forward, "we need to head on over to the high school to meet with them." With that said, the two men turned to leave. Mr. Brewer asked that we stay for a few more minutes.

"I just want to encourage you to be vigilant. Don't go places by yourself. Take your husband or a friend with you. Keep your doors locked. Don't take any unnecessary chances," he said quietly. "I don't mean to scare you. I just want you to be careful. You guys are like family to me and I want you to be safe," he smiled. "Thanks for staying late today. Take care and I'll see you in the morning."

I walked slowly back to my room to get my coat and purse, mulling over the recent turn of events and how they affected me. Mr. Walker, the head custodian was sweeping the hall near my door. As I approached, he stopped and rubbed his hand over his short grey hair. "It sure is a shame about those teachers. I knew Miss Hall. Worked at her school two years ago," he stated matter-of-factly. "She was a real nice lady," he mused. "Say, Miss Carter, do you ever need any work done around your place? I hear you have a dog. I can build a doghouse. Maybe you need some shelves or I can fix cabinets. Anything like that. And I work cheap," he smiled.

A chill ran up my spine. "Uh… no… Mr. Walker. I don't need anything done. But thanks for offering," I sputtered as I opened the door and scurried into my room. I grabbed my things quickly and headed out. "I'll see you tomorrow," I stammered as I practically ran up the hall toward the front door.

By the time I got home, I was shaking so hard I could hardly climb the steps. And it had nothing to do with the chilly wind whipping around me. I fumbled with the key for what seemed like forever before I finally was able to open the door. I slammed it shut behind me, slumped to the floor and hugged my knees. Molly barked excitedly for a minute and then sat down tilting her head from side to side, as she studied me between the slats in the gate.

"I'm sorry girl," I apologized. "I am so edgy over this whole thing. And I know I am over reacting to everything," I picked her up and held her close. She licked my chin and laid her head on my shoulder. "Thank you, baby girl. I guess you need to go outside, don't you?" Her ears perked up and she started wriggling. "OK. Let's go," I put her down, grabbed her leash and headed to the door.

The Birthday Killer

We had just been in the lot a few minutes when I heard a man's voice behind me. "I figured I would find you back here." I jumped and whirled around quickly with a startled yelp to see Sam standing there. He reacted to my frightened response by covering the distance between us in three strides. He put his arms around me as I burst into tears. "Janet, I am so sorry! I did not mean to scare you! Are you alright?" he implored. "You're so pale! You look like all your blood has been drained out of your face. Has something happened?"

I held tightly to him as if my very life depended on it. "Everything is going to be OK. I'm not going to let anything happen to you," he soothed. He stood patiently, holding me firmly until I had gained some semblance of control.

I stepped back and started explaining. "After the meeting... and I was going to... to my room and he stopped me... in the hall and he... he knows Miss Hall and... and he wants to come to... my apartment and... he wants to build a dog... house and he...," the words spilled out in rapid succession between gasping breaths.

"Hold on. Slow down. Who are you talking about?" Sam interrupted me; confusion evident on his face. Then he looked down at Molly who was standing beside me looking up from one to the other of us. "Let's go back inside. I think she is ready and you need to sit down and take a few minutes to settle your nerves." He suggested gently.

"Can I get you a glass of water?" he asked after he had ushered me to the couch. I nodded. He stepped over the gate into the kitchen.

"Oh, you can take that down," I said sheepishly. "I was so panicky that I just picked her up over it."

"I kind of gathered that." The compassion in his smile was reflected in his eyes.

Chapter 12
Monday, February 28

Sam pulled a chair over from the dining table, handed me the glass of water and sat down facing me. "Now, take it slow and tell me what happened," he instructed calmly as I drank.

"OK," I took a deep breath. "After the meeting was over today, I went to my room to get my purse and coat. Mr. Walker, the janitor, was sweeping right outside my room. He stopped when I got close and said how it was a shame about the teachers being killed. He said that he knew Miss Hall. He apparently worked at her school before he was at West." I took another sip of water. My hands were still shaking. "He said he knew I had a dog. And then he asked if he could come over and build a dog house or some shelves or something."

"Did he say anything else?"

"No, I don't think so." I tried to remember. "Oh, he said he worked cheap." Sam tried to hide a little smile. I watched as he mulled over what I had told him. He stroked his chin; obviously trying to decide what to say to me.

"What are you not telling me? You know something that you don't want me to know," I accused, my voice full of panic.

"No, that's not it," he replied quietly. "I just want you to know you are not in this alone. First, let me assure you that Mr. Walker really is just a harmless old man. I do not mean that disrespectfully. He grew up in this community and had his own carpentry shop for many years. He sold it when his only son died in a hunting accident about ten years ago. That is when he started working for the school district and yes, he has been at several different schools during that time. He has done a myriad of odd jobs for teachers all over the district; mostly carpentry related. We have done a thorough investigation on him, and all the custodial help in the district for that matter, and he is absolutely innocent. He really is just a nice older man. And, besides, he has an airtight alibi."

"I feel so stupid," I admitted with embarrassment. "I let my imagination just run away with me; jumping to conclusions; seeing things that aren't really there."

"Don't be so hard on yourself. You are not over reacting," Sam disputed with a gentle voice, reaching over to touch my arm. "You are facing a horrendous scenario. Your very existence is being threatened. Your reactions are perfectly normal under the circumstances."

"And just for the record," he continued, "Mrs. Layne and Miss Martinez are having trouble dealing with all of this, too. You are not the only one. This is very trying for all of you. In fact, I have assigned an officer to each of them who will be the specific one they contact to discuss any of their concerns. That officer will check on them regularly and try to offer some feeling of safety. *You,*" he winked, "are stuck with me."

"Thank you, Sam. You don't know how much that means. I really do appreciate it; even if you did scare me half to death!" I smiled timidly.

"I *am* sorry. I'll try not to do that again," he chuckled. "Can I order us a pizza? It's the least I can do for my unfortunate behavior. And besides, I'm starving!"

"Sure. I think you owe me that much," I laughed.

I brewed a pitcher of ice tea and set the table while we waited for the pizza to arrive. I picked up the poster we had worked on the day before and looked at it. "Sam, I don't think Mrs. Layne has to worry about being a target. South Elementary has already lost one teacher. The only two schools left in the district that haven't had a murder are West Elementary and North Elementary."

Sam came up behind me, reached around and took the poster out of my hands. "No. We are not discussing this right now," he said firmly. "We are going to have a nice, quiet evening. We are going to talk about your childhood, my childhood, Molly or anything else that comes to mind as long as it is NOT related to the case." I turned to face him. "Is that understood?" he asked seriously.

"Yes, sir," I replied quietly looking up at him.

There was a knock on the door and Sam went to get the pizza.

Chapter 13
Wednesday, March 1

March was definitely coming in like a lion. The wind was blowing fiercely as I took Molly out for her morning business. Luckily, it had dried up all the rain from the previous afternoon so we did not have mud to deal with in the back lot. I missed not seeing Sam yesterday; business at work needed his attention so he had to stay late. He had called in the evening to see how my day had gone and promised to see me today. On the third ball toss to Molly, I remembered that I had not gotten the mail yesterday. "That downpour messed us up, didn't it girl. Don't let me forget to check the mail on our way in." She responded with a bark and leaped at the ball catching it in mid-air.

"Way to go, Molly," I exclaimed. "Come on, let's go. I've got bus duty this morning and I can't be late."

I stopped by the mailboxes beside the office. I had three letters; the telephone bill, an advertisement from Gibson's Thrift Store, and a lime green envelope postmarked in Mable, a small town about twenty miles northeast of Lakin. My name was printed neatly on the front. There was no return address. It piqued my interest; something about it seemed vaguely familiar. I took Molly's leash off and hung it on the hook by the door. Dropping the other pieces of mail on the table; I slid my finger under the green flap and opened the envelope. "NOOO!" I screamed as I threw the envelope away from me as if it were burning my hands. A card with purple Irises flew out as it sailed across the room.

I grabbed the telephone and shakily dialed the police department. "I've got to speak to Detective Reynolds," I blurted when the Dispatcher answered the phone.

"I'm sorry. Detective Reynolds is at a meeting. I can take a message and have him return your call when he returns," she replied calmly in her professional business voice.

"No, I need him *now*," I insisted urgently. There was a knock at the door. I froze. Molly ran to the door barking.

The Birthday Killer

"Janet, it's me," Sam's voice called from the other side of the door. I dropped the phone, ran to the door and jerked it open. I pulled him inside pointing to the envelope and card lying in front of the couch. I couldn't speak. I just hid behind him while he went and picked them up.

"Hello? Is everything alright?" The faraway sounding voice on the telephone kept asking. Sam picked it up. "It's me, Beckett. Yeah, everything is OK. If you will let them know, we are running late. Yeah, thanks. I'll check in with you after the meeting." He responded before hanging up.

"I thought you didn't get one of these since you were OK when I called last night." He turned to look at me. "And then, just now when I turned the corner I could see the green when you were going up the stairs. I tried to get here before you opened it." I stared at him, my body shaking uncontrollably. "Did you read it?" he asked.

I jumped back, raising my hands as if to stop him. "No. No," was all I could hoarsely utter. He reached out to take my hand. I pulled away glaring at the envelope.

"Janet, look at me. It's me, Sam. Come sit down on the couch," he instructed. I moved slowly toward the couch, circling to keep my distance from him and the danger he was holding.

He put the offending envelope on the table and came to sit beside me on the couch. He touched my hand and I collapsed into shuddering sobs. He cradled me in his arms, rocking me gently while uttering soothing words. "Everything's OK. I am here. It's going to be all right," he kept repeating.

When I was quiet Sam explained, "Apparently he drove around Monday to three different towns to mail these. They just say to enjoy the extra day you got because it's leap year." After a pause he continued, "I worked on a new addition to our security plan last night and I told Mrs. Layne and Miss Martinez that we would meet this morning to discuss it. They are pretty devastated over this, too."

Suddenly my mind snapped to attention. "What time is it?" I sat straight up. "I'm supposed to be at school for bus duty." I hopped up. Sam reached out and grabbed my arm pulling me back onto the couch.

"No you don't. I already worked it out with Mr. Nicholas for the three of you to have substitutes for today. I had Beckett call Mr. Brewer to let him know we would be late. You have all the time you need to process this and get a handle on it before we go to the meeting. So, just sit here and try to relax."

Molly nudged my leg with her nose and gave a little whimper. She looked up at me with worried eyes; her ears drooping. "Oh, Sweetheart, I'm sorry this is scary for you, too." I reached down, picked her up, and let her lay on my lap. I looked at Sam. "Could you do what you were doing?" I asked timidly.

"What's that?" he asked.

"Just hold me," I replied shyly.

"I can do that," he smiled as he gently pulled me close.

Chapter 14
Wednesday, March 1

Mrs. Layne and Miss Martinez were seated in their customary places when Sam and I entered the room. The two ladies stood up and we all three embraced. "Oh, most precious Heavenly Father," Mrs. Layne prayed fervently. "Keep us safe and give us strength to get through this."

"Amen," Miss Martinez and I said in unison. As we sat down, I noticed, for the first time, that there were three other people standing to the left side of the room.

"Good morning," Sam nodded at the new comers. "Ladies, I want to introduce you to the next step of our security plan. For the next few weeks or however long is necessary, these officers will be in your classrooms. You can tell the students that they are Student Teachers or Teacher's Aides or whatever makes you feel the most comfortable. I probably wouldn't mention that they are your bodyguards; no need to alarm the students," he smiled. "Mrs. Layne, this is Sargent Jerry Monroe. Miss Martinez, this is Officer Mark Davis. Miss Carter, this is Officer Linda Chase. You will have time at the end of this meeting to discuss with each other how you will work things out. You can have them just sit in your classroom or you can put them to work and make them earn their keep," he smiled.

"In addition to these guys," he continued, "we have also assigned a uniformed officer to your campus. Now, Miss Martinez, you already have one at your school so you will not be getting another one. Their job will be to be visible on campus and make regular rounds of the buildings on site."

There was a quick tap at the door and Mr. Nicholas stepped into the office and quickly scanned the room. "I just wanted to drop by and let you ladies know that we are doing everything possible to keep you safe." He smiled at the three of us. "If there is anything else you need, just let me know. I will get with Detective Reynolds to see how to make it happen." With a nod and a wave, he was back out the door.

"OK..." Sam cleared his throat. "Now, about our latest contact from... I'm going to call him Mr. X," Sam continued. "You each got a card mailed from a different location within a twenty mile radius of Lakin. I suspect he knows we are stepping things up and he is playing with us. What I am going to say is not something you want to hear and I am truly sorry for that. I believe he is watching to see how we react and handle whatever he throws at us. In addition, most likely, things are going to get a lot worse before they get better. By that, I mean that I expect to see more activity from him toward each of you. In the three previous incidents his communication was only with the victims; not the others sharing birthdays within each month. This is a game to him; a mind game more than anything else, but we do not have to play by his rules. We will do our best to stay one-step ahead of him. Unfortunately, we do not have any idea where or how he will strike again. We do not know if all of you will be contacted by him or only one of you. That is why we are putting officers in your rooms and on your campuses. Our job is to keep you safe and that is what we will do. Let me encourage you to reach out to any of us if you have any qualms or concerns about this atrocious situation."

Sam paused, looking at each of us before plunging into his next statement. He took a deep breath. "Miss Martinez, we will be focusing extra security on you since your birthday is the first one this month." Her hands clenched the arms of the chair; her knuckles turning white. Her breathing became shallow and rapid. "That is not to say that we think you are the target. We do not know which one of you is the target. I wish I did. It would make this a lot easier. We have been examining the specifics of the previous cases and we have, in fact, determined how *each* of you *could* be the next target as well as how each one of you is *not* a target at all." Sam shook his head. "We will continue to scrutinize every detail to try and find some answers."

"Your uh... new best friend," he nodded toward the officers standing behind us, "will meet you in the parking lot every morning when you arrive and walk you to your car when you leave at the end of the day. They will be with you every moment in between. They are here for your protection... yes ...but more importantly for your peace of mind. You each still have your contact person who will keep you informed of any new developments as soon as we are aware of them, as well as the undercover agents who shadow your every move. Even though you do not see them, rest assured; they are there. You have someone watching you twenty-four hours a day." He paused for a moment. "There is no way I can fully understand how you ladies must feel. I know this is extremely difficult for you to come to terms with; to try to comprehend this whole situation. I just want you to know that I am doing everything in my power to make sure you are taken care of and protected – physically and mentally," he said compassionately.

"Now for the good news," Sam said cheerily. "You have the day off! Sort of," he laughed. "You need to spend some time this afternoon with your partner and get to know each other. Discuss your classroom situations… how they will fit in the scheme of things… what you need from them. You can use a table in the library here, you can go back to your own campus or you can go out for lunch. Where you spend the next few hours is strictly up to you. I have business to tend to at the office," he glanced at me apologetically, "but you are now free to go. Please remember that we are here for you. We are a team and together we will beat Mr. X at his own game," he added encouragingly.

We stood and turned to greet our new partners as Sam slipped out the door. Part of me went with him. Linda Chase, a twenty-nine year old, five foot six, red head had been with the Department for six years. She was not a local. She had moved here, like many of us, for the job. She had started out as a crossing guard near North Elementary and had moved up a few ranks to where she now had her own beat. She had worked hard to prove herself in a man's world and was making progress little by little.

I took "Miss Linda", as I would introduce her, to meet my students. I could hear a big commotion in my room as we neared the door. "You can't play with that over here," the substitute was saying in frustration.

"Can, too," came the loud, sassy reply from Tina. I opened the door to find Tina and Randy rolling purple play dough between two triangular blocks in the puzzle area.

"What is going on in here?" I demanded. Everyone stopped and stared. You could hear a pin drop. And then when they realized it was me, they all rushed toward me. "No. Wait just a minute," I held up my hands. They stopped. "I cannot believe this. Mrs. Taylor," I nodded at the sub, "has come to help me when I could not be here and this is how you behave? This is totally unacceptable. Tina, how do we talk to adults? Randy, why do you have the play dough and the blocks in the puzzle area? Where do those things belong? Donna, we do not use finger-paint on the home living table. This makes me very sad. Every one of you knows the rules and how we behave in this classroom." Tina walked over to Mrs. Taylor and pulled on her skirt. "I be sorry," she hung her head. Mrs. Taylor gave her a hug.

"Now, you guys," I changed the subject. "I want you to meet Miss Linda. She is going to be spending some time in our class and I hope you will show her how good you can be." Ronnie galloped over, got off his imaginary horse and shook hands. Dave gave his opinion from the library center. "You pretty!" he exclaimed. Linda laughed and said thanks.

"OK. We have to go back to our meeting now. I expect you to have all this mess cleaned up before you go home," I pointed around the room. "And I hope Mrs. Taylor can give me a good report about your behavior for the rest of the day. I will see you in the morning."

"Hope you are up for the challenge," I teased Linda as we walked back toward the office. "You may be asking for a reassignment."

"I think I can handle it," she replied with a chuckle. "Where do you want to go eat lunch? Do you like pizza?"

Chapter 15
Thursday, March 2

The front page of the Lakin Daily Messenger boasted a picture of Sam and Mr. Nicholas at the press conference they had yesterday afternoon. I read the accompanying story with interest.

POLICE AND SCHOOLS BAND TOGETHER FOR PROTECTION OF TEACHERS

The Lakin Police Department in conjunction with the Lakin Independent School District released a statement yesterday afternoon at a press conference held at the Lakin ISD Administration Building. Police Detective Sam Reynolds, who is in charge of the on-going investigation of the recent teacher homicides, indicated that security at each of the schools has been ramped up with additional patrols around the campuses throughout the school day. He further specified that evidence in the three recent slayings of teachers in the Lakin ISD indicated these crimes were perpetrated by the same person. Reynolds confirmed that the crimes are believed to possibly be committed by a serial killer.

Reynolds established that the three victims were killed within a few days of their birthdays. "There are no identified suspects at this time," acknowledged Reynolds.

When questioned about the possibility of any current teachers being in danger, Reynolds stated," Yes, there are several teachers we are providing specific security measures for at this time." He refused to give the identities of those teachers.

George Nicholas, Superintendent of the Lakin ISD stated, "We are working closely with the local law enforcement to ensure that all of our schools are safe. None of the students in our care are in any danger."

There was nothing in the article I didn't already know. I tossed the ball for Molly a few times and got ready to go to school. "I don't dread going today," I told Molly as I fixed her gate. "I guess having Linda in the room with me is a good idea. At least she will know what to do if something happens!" Molly barked her agreement. Remembering the mess I had seen the afternoon before, I wondered what I would find when I got to school.

"It's hard to 'meet you at your car' when you walk to school," Linda informed me with a smile when I arrived at the front door. "At least I can watch you coming down the street." She added with a shrug.

I was relieved to see that my room was back to normal. Everything had been returned to its proper center and all the messes cleaned up. The note on my desk from Mrs. Taylor said the kids had been on their best behavior for the rest of the day.

Linda had a natural gift for working with special needs children. She fit right in with our schedule of activities and the day flew by. I enjoyed my walk home after school; the warm sun felt good on my face. The blustery wind had a little sting to it but I didn't mind. It was a beautiful day and I was relishing it.

Molly, as usual, was eager to go outside when I got home. As we were coming down the stairs to go to the lot behind the apartments, Sam drove up. "Good afternoon," he called. "Mind if I tag along?"

"Of course you can! We would love to have you," I beamed; my heart giving a little leap at seeing him.

"You are in a good mood," he noted.

"Thank you for putting Linda in my room. Having her there even just one day really has helped. I don't know how to explain it but I guess I would say... I feel safe. And besides, she is really good with the kids!"

Sam nodded with a strange little smile. "I thought she would be a good match for you; the only one I would trust in there."

Molly raced around the lot a few times pausing to bark at the bushes in the far corner. She returned expectantly, jumping up and down, ready for her ball. Sam and I talked between tosses. "How did you like my picture?" he asked; posing and trying to look important.

"I was thinking about asking for your autograph. I've never known a celebrity before," I teased.

"Just trying to do my job," he smiled. I loved the way his eyes twinkled when he was being playful. "Keeping the people happy." He flung the ball again. "I thought I would see if you wanted to go out for a burger," he added a little more seriously.

"Sounds good. A girl's got to eat," I laughed. My laughter turned into a gasp as I watched Molly trotting back to us with something green in her mouth.

Sam stooped to take the plastic ball from her. It had "I like green better" written around the center." Instantly Sam took off like a shot toward the back corner of the lot. Molly ran after him but I called her back. He disappeared through the bushes and was gone for a few minutes while I stood glued to the spot, paralyzed with fear. When he returned he handed Molly's blue ball back to me. "He got away through the gate at the other end," he reported angrily. "There was nobody in sight. He probably left as soon as he gave her the ball. Didn't leave any clear prints in the dirt either," he added.

"Oh, Sam," I quivered, tears streaming down my face, "I can't... bring Molly... back here anymore! He's watching us!" I pleaded for an answer, "What am I going to do? It's not safe for us here."

"We will work it out. I promise," he put his arm around my shoulder. "Let's go in." He guided me gently toward the apartment.

Sam pulled the green ball out of his pocket as he shut the door behind us. "It's the same writing as the notes," he observed as he studied the ball.

"You can take that with you. I don't want it here," I shuddered. "And please, take *this* with you, too." I picked up the green envelope and its contents from the table with two fingers as if it was going to bite me and held it out to him. Solemnly he took it from me, folded the envelope and put it along with the green ball in his pocket.

"I wish I could make all this go away for you," Sam said softly as he hugged me close. I relished the feeling of his arms around me; I could feel their strength. I felt safe and secure.

He pulled back, "Think you are up for that burger?"

"Oh Sam, he's watching me. Some crazy, deranged, lunatic is spying on me! That makes me feel so... I don't know... so... violated! I don't want to go *anywhere*!" I sat down on the couch, clasped my hands under my chin and rocked back and forth.

"I understand," he said in a quiet, compassionate voice. "But you can't let him beat you down. You've got to show him that you are tougher than that." Sam encouraged as he sat down on the couch beside me and took my hands in his. "We won't go anywhere in town. How about if we drive to Channelwick? It's not that far and The Burger Barn there has the best malts this side of the Mississippi River. What do you say? Please? You need a change of scenery," he implored in a compelling voice.

"OK," I agreed reluctantly. "But you're driving," I added teasingly with a sly smile. Suddenly, I felt almost giddy.

"That's my girl!" he beamed. "I'm glad you are getting you sense of humor back." I smiled and thumped him on the arm.

A little over half way to Channelwick, Sam caught me looking in the side mirror. "There's no one following us," he said reassuringly. "I've been watching. Give me a *little* credit," he feigned offence. I responded with a heavy sigh and a slight smile. It was difficult but I resisted the urge to look again. He reached over and squeezed my hand. "I'm really glad you decided to come," he said quietly giving me a special smile.

There was no waiting when we arrived. We were immediately ushered to a small table against the wall. "What? You don't have a special booth here?" I teased.

"I don't come here that often. Have to watch my boyish figure, you know," he joked back, patting his midsection. "Their malts could be addicting."

While we were waiting for our burgers and malts, Sam rubbed his chin, obviously deep in thought. After a few minutes he pointed at me and said, "I've been thinking. I'll come over in the morning and take Molly out for you. What time do you usually do that? And then I will assign an officer to cover that back gate in the afternoon while you are out there."

"We usually go out sometime between six thirty and six forty-five in the morning; after school, of course. And then again around nine thirty or ten; right before bed time," I responded.

"Check. I can have him cover that too, if I'm not around to do it," he said thoughtfully. "Will that be OK?" he asked. "Does it work for you?"

"Yeah, that will be fine, I guess." I replied.

Our order arrived and after a brief prayer of blessing, we dug in. Once again, Sam was right. The chocolate malt was absolutely delicious. Moreover, the burgers weren't too bad either.

Chapter 16
Friday, March 3

Sam arrived at six thirty-one Friday morning. When I opened the door, he was standing there holding a box of donuts. "I brought breakfast," he announced. "Hopefully you have some coffee to go with these." He set the box on the table.

"I was just putting it on. It should be ready by the time you two get back." I smiled and nodded at Molly who was waiting by the door. He hooked her leash and headed out the door. Before he pulled it shut, "Sam," I called. He stuck his head back in the door with a questioning look. "Thank you," I smiled.

"My pleasure," he smiled back; his eyes shining.

I hummed as I got the coffee cups ready. "Thank you God, for Sam," I whispered a quick prayer of thanksgiving. "How many men would come over early in the morning to take a dog out for a walk, job or no job?" I said to the coffee pot as I waited for it to finish percolating. He had insisted on taking her out last night after he had checked my apartment when we got back from the Burger Barn. "That's a man dedicated to his job," I said to the sugar bowl and creamer as I put them on the table.

"We're back," he laughed as Molly came bounding in the door. "She certainly has a lot of energy for so early in the morning," he alleged. He bounced her ball toward the bedroom and she went scrambling after it. "Coffee smells good," he said as he pulled out a chair and sat down. I poured us both a cup and joined him at the table.

Sam drove me to school and promised to pick me up at the end of the day. Linda smiled broadly when she saw us drive into the parking lot. "I see you were brave enough to come back for day two," I teased.

"Yes, but I had to drive myself," she responded with raised eyebrows and waved at Sam as he drove off. We both laughed and headed inside. I filled her in on the events of the evening before. She listened with interest, shaking her head in astonishment. Her expression changed when I got to the part about the Burger Barn and Sam taking Molly out to do her business.

"He's sweet on you," she stated.

"No he isn't," I denied. "I am just a job to him. He's only doing what he has to do until all this is over."

"I think you better rethink that theory," she advised with a serious nod. I could feel myself blushing and I was not totally surprised to realize that I liked the idea of her suspicions.

Our time with the students went smoothly. I was again very impressed with the way Linda related to the kids. They loved her. She was a natural. "You know, if you ever want to change professions, you would make a great teacher," I told her.

The closer to the end of the day; the slower the time went. I kept checking the clock. I did not think four o'clock would ever get here. As promised, Sam was waiting when we waked out the door. My heart fluttered and a feeling of delight surged through me.

We both took Molly for her afternoon romp in the lot. We sat on the bench nearest the gate we entered and watched while she ran around like a tornado. She stopped at the far corner and barked at the bushes. Every muscle in my body tensed and I held my breath in panic.

"It's OK," Sam soothed. "It's just my guy." I let out a long slow breath. "Here, girl," he called as he threw her ball. "Mrs. Layne got a message last night, too," he informed me.

"Really?" I asked hesitantly.

"She and her husband went to a movie and there was a note on the car when they came out," he expounded. "It said 'Good to be making memories while there is still time.' They went back in the theater and called her contact. Scary time for her too," he added sympathetically. He tossed the ball again.

"What about Miss Martinez?" I inquired.

"Nothing," he stated frankly.

"I'm glad for her. This is so bizarre, Sam. There has to be some way we can figure out who this guy is...surely there is something. I was looking at the chart and the pictures..."

"I'm going to take those away from you," he threatened in an almost teasing manner.

"No, I'm OK with them, really. However, I look at them and I just feel like there is something I am missing. There has got to be something...some clue...some detail that we just aren't getting," I mused. We sat silently for a few minutes; Sam tossing the ball for Molly when she brought it back.

"Sam, I have a question. If someone is supposed to be watching us 'twenty-four hours a day', how can Mr. X put a note on their car and not get caught?"

"Fair question." He thought for a moment. "Let me explain it this way. The officer that is assigned to you will keep you in his sight at all times. If you go to Gibson's or Safeway or anywhere else, that officer is in the store with you. He is going to be checking your surroundings to be sure that there is no threat to you," he paused to see if I understood.

"I'm with you. Go ahead," I told him affirmatively.

"If one of you is with your contact, like I'm here now, then the undercover officer will not have to be watching you. We communicate with each other over our police radios to know when the surveillance responsibility is handed off to the next man." His brow furrowed. "Is that clear? Or did I just make a mess of it? I don't want to insult you by sounding like I am talking down to you because I am definitely not trying to do that," he rambled with an obvious look of concern on his face.

"No, you're good," I assured him. "Basically you're saying the officer was in the theater watching Mrs. Layne so there was no one keeping tabs on the car."

"Uh, yeah. That's exactly what I said," he smiled sheepishly.

We watched as Molly, tail wagging, disappeared into the bushes at the far end. In a minute, her ball came sailing out of the mass of leaves with Molly in hot pursuit.

"So, if he doesn't have to be here when you are here, why is he here?" I nodded in the direction of the far corner.

"I told him to stick around so you could see that he is on duty when you are out here. So if I'm *not* here then you know he *is* here." I laughed as he shrugged his shoulders in mock confusion.

Sam was quiet for a moment. "Not to change the subject but, do you like Chicken Fried Steak? Martin's Restaurant cooks up a real humdinger. Their crust is perfect, the meat is melt-in-your-mouth tender and the cream gravy is out of this world."

I looked at him in disbelief. "Do you know the specialty for *every* restaurant or eating joint in the county?"

"Pretty much," he admitted matter-of-factly. "Nobody cooks at my place," he shrugged. "I have to eat somewhere. Oh, and while we are on the topic of eating, are you going to invite me over for lunch on Sunday?"

I started laughing. "I guess so. What is it you think you want to eat?"

"Meatloaf," he said without hesitation. "Haven't found a place that has decent meatloaf."

"Oh great, no pressure there," I just shook my head. "Meatloaf it is."

Chapter 17
Saturday, March 4

Sam called just after five o'clock to let me know that he would not be able to take Molly out. The sun was not even up yet. He did not, or would not, elaborate on some issue that came up and he had to go straight to the office. He assured me that I would have two people watching while I was out with Molly. It was not as good as if he was there but it did give me some sense of security.

I laid in bed thinking about dinner last night with Sam. Martin's was a nicer restaurant with crisp, white polished cotton tablecloths and a flickering candle surrounded by fresh flowers in the center of each table. At Sam's request, we had been seated at a table in the corner. After placing our order, Sam informed me, "No talking about business. It's just you and me." I smiled at him and between the dim lighting and glowing candlelight, I felt like I was in some wonderful dreamland. We talked about his early years and some of the mischief he and his brother got into and the trouble they caused their parents. When our food arrived, Sam reached for my hand before saying grace.

Molly jumped on the bed, breaking my reverie. "Hey girl, is it time for you to go out already?" I looked at the clock. Six forty-two. "OK, I guess it is business as usual, isn't it?" I scratched her ears. We went out back and I watched the bushes to see if there was any indication that someone was there. Molly paused only briefly, wagging her tail and then scampered on her way.

After breakfast, I got out Mom's recipe for meatloaf. My plan was to cook everything this afternoon and then put it in the oven on low in the morning to warm so it would be ready when I got home from church. I made a list of items I needed and headed out to the grocery store. The parking lot was almost empty. Two lone cars were parked near the entrance. As I wheeled my cart through the produce area Miss Martinez rounded the corner headed in my direction.

"Good morning," she greeted with a pensive smile. I was taken aback by her haggard appearance. I hoped my face did not reveal the shock I felt at seeing her. "My sister is coming today to spend the week with me. I couldn't sleep so I figured I may as well get my shopping done. What brings you out so early?"

"I was up and didn't have anything else to do," I smiled back. "It will be good for you to have some company."

"I am so scared," she admitted. "I am a nervous wreck! I can't sleep. I can't eat. I'm OK at school since Officer Davis is there but when I get home…" she shook her head. "I hate being alone. So, Pam decided to take a week of vacation to come stay with me. Her bus should get here about one fifteen. I am excited for her to be coming."

"I know what you mean. The hardest part *is* being at home alone. I'm glad she is able to come." I responded and bid her farewell. I checked off the items on my list as I finished shopping. I paused in front of the frozen desserts. Nothing looked good; I decided I would just make brownies.

The meatloaf was cooling, the brownies were in the oven and I had just covered the bowl of mashed potatoes with foil when Sam called. "Just checking in. Everything going OK?" he asked casually.

"So far, so good," I answered. "How has your day been?"

"Long!" he groaned. "What are you doing for supper?"

"I'm going to have a grilled cheese sandwich and a cup of tomato soup."

"That sounds good. I just have a little bit to finish on this report and I'll be right there. I'll take two sandwiches," he informed me with enthusiasm.

"OK," I laughed. "See you soon."

Between bites of his second sandwich, Sam told me about his day. "Dispatch got a call at four twenty-two this morning from a man claiming to know who Mr. X is and he wanted to give his story to 'the one in charge.' Since I'm the lucky one to be that person I had to go in and wait for him to call back; which he didn't bother to do until eighteen minutes after six." He said in exasperation.

"So, you know who he is! Did you catch him?" I asked excitedly. "Who is it?"

Sam held up his hand and shook his head while he took a drink of tomato soup. "According to the informant, who chose to remain anonymous, it's Mr. Layne"

"WHAT!" I exclaimed.

"Yep. Supposedly, Layne killed the three teachers because he wanted to kill his wife and wanted it to look like someone else did it. The man said there was evidence at the Lakin Daily Messenger office. Wanting to follow every possible lead, even those we suspect are bogus; we went to the newspaper office. When we got there, we found the front of the building covered with black and red graffiti accusations. Turned out to be a disgruntled Copy Editor Layne fired last month trying to get revenge."

"Do you think Mr. Layne has anything to do with the murders?" I asked him doubtfully.

"No." He shook his head. "We had already eliminated him as a suspect before we even started meeting with the three of you."

"Oh, that's really disappointing," I mused. "I mean not that it isn't Mr. Layne, I'm glad for that! I just wish we knew who it was so this could all be over."

"I know," he squeezed my hand. "I wish it was over, too." He paused a moment and then continued. "What did you and Miss Martinez have to talk about this morning?"

"How do you know I talked to Miss Martinez?" I asked in astonishment.

Sam laughed. "You know I have spies everywhere!" he teased.

"She said her sister was coming to stay with her this week. This is really taking a toll on her; bless her heart. She looked bad," I relayed sorrowfully. "Sam," I looked intently at him. "Thank you for spending time with me. It really does help. Does she and her contact not keep in touch that much?" I asked.

"Not really. She didn't seem interested in having him around. Not sure why," he responded. "Hey, did I smell brownies when I came in?" he brightened.

"Yes, you did but they are for dessert tomorrow."

"We can't try them out tonight?" he asked with a crestfallen look; his shoulders slumping. I laughed and went to the kitchen to get him a brownie. "I can tell you one thing," he announced when I returned to the table. "I know where to get the best grilled cheese. I won't be going to the City Café for that anymore."

"Oh, so now I'm your short order cook?" I put my hands on my hips.

Sam just grinned and took a bite of the brownie.

Chapter 18
Sunday, March 5

Sam arrived bright and early Sunday morning and insisted on taking Molly out for her morning routine before church. I put everything for lunch in the oven and was ready to go when they returned. "Sam, you don't have to go with me to my church. I feel bad keeping you from going where you usually go," I said. "I'm not afraid to be there by myself. You can go to your church if you prefer."

"That's not why I am going," he responded, looking wounded. "Or at least, it's not the *only* reason." He winked. "I understand what you meant when you said you felt like you were home there. There is definitely a special feeling of belonging; being where you are supposed to be. It only took one visit to make that determination. I like it there."

"Oh, Sam, I'm sorry. I did not mean you were not welcome. I just don't want you to feel like you have to go because of me; because you are my contact."

"Well," he replied, "I might have started out going because of you; which I might say is not a bad reason, but now I'm going because I *want* to go. It is where I want to worship." He smiled softly.

Pastor Jenkins brought a moving message on trusting God and allowing Him to lead us safely through the tough times. "God wants to fight your battles," he told us as he expounded on specific verses from the books of Psalms and Proverbs.

"You sure are quiet," Sam said on the ride home.

"I was just thinking about the sermon. I do not have enough faith. If I really trusted Him I wouldn't be so afraid," I berated myself.

"I beg to differ," he disagreed as he pulled into a parking space in front of my apartments. He switched off the key and turned to face me. "Even Jesus prayed that if there was some other way than for Him to be crucified. It is not wrong to be afraid. You are facing an unidentified assailant. Your life is being threatened for no logical reason. Your whole routine is being turned up-side down," he counted on his fingers as he continued the list. "You are at the mercy of something or someone who is totally unpredictable. You don't know when or where the next unsettling blow is coming from."

Tears ran down my cheeks as I fidgeted with my hands in my lap. Sam reached over and put his hand under my chin lifting my face; our eyes locked. "You have every right to be afraid. But that doesn't mean you don't have faith," he said gently. "And trust, well… You either trust Him or you don't. There is no in-between."[1] Sam quietly sang the chorus from a familiar hymn.

"Trust and obey, for there's no other way
To be happy in Jesus, but to trust and obey."[2]

We sat quietly for several minutes before he got out and came around to open my door.

Sam and Molly headed downstairs to take care of business while I set the table and finished making the tomato gravy to go with the meatloaf. "If it tastes half as good as it smells," he observed as he hung up Molly's leash, "I'm going to be making a pig of myself." Molly barked and spun in a circle as if to say she agreed with him. We laughed at her and sat down at the table.

After his first bite of meatloaf, Sam looked at me with a big smile of pure delight. "My search is over! I can stop looking for the best meatloaf in the state. You have it right here!" He exclaimed. "This is delicious!"

"You are too funny," I responded with a laugh.

"I'm serious. Can I take some home so I can make a sandwich for lunch tomorrow?"

"Of course, if you really want some," I laughed. "Do I need to make the sandwich for you?"

"No, that's OK." He tried to look serious. "I can do sandwiches. That's about all I can do but I'm good with making my own."

"I don't know what to think of you, Sam Reynolds!" I countered.

"I don't care what you think of me," he smiled, "as long as you think of me."

---

[1] i can't knit, thegirls@icantknit.com, Used by permission.
[2] Trust and Obey, John H. Sammis, Public Domain

Chapter 19
Monday, March 6

Monday morning was cold and soggy. The rain had started just after midnight and continued all night long. Molly was not excited about going out in the deluge and wasted no time in the back lot. We were back in the apartment in record time. Because of the rain, I decided to drive the short distance to school.

Linda met me at the front door of the school. "We need this rain but I kind of wish it would let up for a little while," she greeted.

"You got that right," I agreed. "The kids will be wild if we have to stay in all day. And from the looks of it, I would say we better come up with Plan B for recess time," I warned.

We had just finished setting out the new materials for the week in the Art center when the bell rang and Randy came bounding in the door. "My baby Carter," he crooned, laying his head on my arm.

"I love you, too Randy," I patted his back. "It's good to see you this morning. Let's get your coat off and hang it up."

"Look!" he demanded. With a flourish, he pulled a lime green envelope out of his coat pocket.

"Oh!" I jumped back in horror.

Linda rushed over. "I'll take it for her, Randy."

"NO! Carter," he insisted, thrusting it at me; obviously pleased to be the bearer of such a treasure.

I reached out and took the revolting article; my hands shaking noticeably. "Thank you, Randy," I replied weakly. "Go hang your coat up." As soon as he turned away, I handed the envelop to Linda.

"You need to sit down," she directed with concern. "You don't look so good. Take some deep breaths."

I sank onto the nearest chair; my whole body trembling. I tried to steady my breath and calm my racing heart.

"How in the world did he get this?" Linda questioned.

"Randy," I called him over to the kidney shaped table. "Thank you for the pretty envelope. Where did you get it?" I asked.

"My Carter," he beamed.

"Yes, I know it is for me. Did you find it somewhere?"

"My Carter," he insisted.

"Did somebody give it to you?"

"My Carter!" he exclaimed in frustration.

"It's alright, Randy. Thank you. You can pick a center to play in for now." I instructed. I looked at Linda. "I'm going to the office to call his mom. Maybe she knows something about it."

"Good idea. I'll check in with Reynolds when you get back," she responded. "Unless you want to call him while you're in the office," she suggested.

"No, you can call him. I don't think I can keep it together if I talk to him." I exhaled slowly. "Be right back."

I used the phone in Mr. Brewer's office. He was at the Administration Building for a Principal's meeting. I was glad for the privacy. "Hello Mrs. Perkins. This is Janet Carter. I need to ask you a quick question. Randy came in with a green envelope this morning. Do you have any idea where he might have gotten it?" I queried hopefully.

"Yes," she replied without hesitation. "A man came jogging up when I was letting him out of the car. He asked Randy to give it to you."

I felt like someone had thrown a glass of ice water in my face. I could not move. I could not breathe. I could not speak.

"Hello? Miss Carter, are you there?" Mrs. Perkins sounded alarmed.

"I'm sorry," I stammered. "I got distracted for a minute. Did you know the man? What did he look like?" I asked cautiously.

"I really couldn't tell you. I think he had a beard. I did not get a good look at him. He was wearing one of those gray sweat suits and he had the hood pulled way up over his head but I am pretty sure I have never seen him before. He wasn't anybody I know."

"OK, thanks. I had better get back to class. I just wanted to check." I ended the call. When I returned to the room, I filled Linda in on what I had learned and she headed to the office. I sat at the table in a fog; unable to concentrate on the activity around me. He had contact with one of my students. He knew who they were, or at least he knew one of them. Did that mean my students were in danger?

"Carter, I need you." Tina tugged at my sleeve. She was trying to put on the pink ballerina dress that had somehow become all twisted around. I straightened it out and helped her slip it on over her head. She pirouetted back to the Home Living center

Linda was gone for a while before she returned to the room looking grim. "What's going on?" I asked with concern.

"It took longer than I expected to get hold of Reynolds. He is meeting with the three Principals and the Superintendent this morning. Nicholas had a flat tire and was running late so they aren't finished with their

58

conference or he would be on his way over here. But the big news is," she paused. "You *all* got cards. Same message. Same method of delivery."

I took a deep breath. "What does it say?" I asked, not really wanting to know.

"Spring will be here soon. Will you be around to see it?"

I shivered.

"You should go home," Linda suggested.

"I can't. It is too late to get a sub. I need to be here with my kids. Besides, I really don't feel like being alone right now."

"I told Reynolds you would say that," she commented. "I can handle the class. He said he would come pick you up as soon as he could."

"He doesn't need to do that. He's too busy with things a lot more important than being bothered with me," I protested.

"I don't think he was planning on asking your permission," she countered.

An hour and a half later Mrs. Post opened the door. "You need to get your things. There is someone in the office to take you home," she said compassionately.

"But I need to stay…"

"I was told to accept no excuses," she interrupted.

"I hate to say it," Linda jumped in, "but you're not really here anyway. You didn't even notice when Dave got the records out of the Listening center to use for plates in Home Living."

"He did what?" I gasped in astonishment.

"I've got it covered," she assured me. "Get out of here."

Sam was waiting just outside the office. Tears welled up in my eyes and spilled down my cheeks. He put his arm around my shoulders and steered me out of the building to his waiting car.

"I'll come back later and get your car," Sam said as he buckled his seatbelt. "I'm going to get you settled in first."

Molly barked excitedly when we opened the door. Sam took down the gate so she could move freely about the apartment. With tears still flowing, I apologized. "I'm sorry I am so much trouble." Sam moved to stand in front of me. "You have way too much to do to be bothered with me. I…"

Sam put his finger to my lips; his eyes stared into mine. "I take care of what is important to me," he said, his voice husky with emotion. He pulled me into his arms. "You're trembling," he observed. "Why don't you go lay down? Get some rest."

"I don't want to lay down. You'll leave and there is no way I can settle down to rest." I responded through my tears.

"I am not leaving," he assured me tenderly. "Come on then; let's just sit on the couch for a while." Molly jumped up to snuggle between Sam and the arm of the couch. I sat on the other side; my head on his shoulder. He locked his arms around me and began to sing softly.

"When peace, like a river, attendeth my way,
When sorrows like sea billows roll;
Whatever my lot, Thou hast taught me to say,
It is well; it is well with my soul.

"It is well with my soul,
It is well; it is well with my soul.

Though Satan should buffet, though trials should come,
Let this blest assurance control,
That Christ hath regarded my helpless estate,
And hath shed His own blood for my soul.

"It is well with my soul,
It is well; it is well with my soul."[3]

I relaxed in the beauty of the old hymn and the soothing sound of his voice. "Oh Sam, I love that song," I whispered. "It's one of my favorites. Thank you for singing to me." His arms gave me a gentle squeeze. I felt safe and peaceful for the first time in what seemed like forever. I drifted off to sleep while he sang the remaining stanzas of the hymn.

I awoke to the aroma of meatloaf. I was lying on the couch with the blanket from the end of my bed covering me. I could hear Sam humming in the kitchen. "What are you doing in there?" I asked.

He poked his head around the corner. "Warming up some lunch. Hope you don't mind; I left mine at the office. Do you like meatloaf sandwiches?" he smiled.

"Actually, I do," I responded.

"Good. You just stay right there and I will have them ready in a minute." He set up two TV trays in front of the couch and put a glass of

---

[3] "It Is Well With My Soul, Horatio G. Spafford, Public Domain

milk on each. He retreated to the kitchen and returned shortly with two plates; each containing a sandwich and some potato chips.

"How did Mrs. Layne and Miss Martinez handle their messages today?" I asked.

"Miss Martinez is going home," he paused. "Or I should say to her parents' home. She and her sister are leaving today. She is not planning to come back until this is over. Mr. Nicholas was very supportive of her decision. He promised that her position would be waiting for her when she returns. Mrs. Layne took the rest of the day off. Her husband picked her up and took her home."

"Did their students' bring the notes to them?"

"No, he apparently just stopped random students who were going in the building and asked if they would deliver it to them."

"What about my students, Sam. Do you think they are in any danger?" I asked with concern. "Obviously Mr. X knows Randy is in my room. I don't think I would ever get over it if something happened to one of my kids because of me."

"Clearly, we don't know who we're dealing with but I don't see him going after the students. I think he just has some kind of issues with adult women. He has really stepped things up this time but it still seems to just be directed at the three of you. He's bound to make some mistake and show his hand with all this extra activity," he mused hopefully. "That's enough about all of that," Sam said with determination. "Do you have any games we can play?"

"I have Monopoly, dominoes, Scrabble, cards ..."

"Let's do Scrabble. I haven't played that in years," he confessed.

We had just started the third game when Dispatch called and Sam had to leave. When I walked him to the door, he pulled me into his arms and held me tightly. "I really hate to be leaving," he said and gently kissed the top of my head.

Chapter 20
Tuesday, March 7

If it hadn't been for needing to take Molly out I wouldn't have gotten out of bed at all. For the first time in my life, I really did not want to go to school. Sam arranged for Linda to pick me up because he had other matters that needed his attention. I was relieved that the morning at school went routinely. I was not sure how many more surprises I could take. By the end of the day, I felt like things were getting back to normal.

After switching out materials and setting up the room for Wednesday morning, Linda and I headed out. "You want to go get some Pizza?" she asked. "I think we need some girl time. And besides, I want to hear how your day was with Reynolds yesterday," she added with a smile. "I hear he didn't show up at work until after five o'clock!"

"OK," I laughed, "but I need to run home first and take Molly out."

The buffet at the Pizza Palace offered a wide variety of fresh, hot pizza. The accompanying salad bar was small but had a decent number of ingredients to choose from to make a pretty good salad. We settled in a booth by the front windows; Linda taking the side facing the door. The waitress brought our drinks over. After a little small talk about things at school, Linda remarked, "Now for the scoop on yesterday. I want to hear every detail! The guys in the department are counting on me"

"What's that supposed to mean? Why does anybody care what happened?" I questioned with a chuckle.

"We are talking about Reynolds," she said informatively. "The man who is at work by seven every morning and doesn't leave until after six thirty or seven in the evening. Sometimes it is after eight o'clock before he goes home. That happens like clockwork, Monday through Friday and many times on Saturday." She paused to take a breath. "Now, he comes in later; leaves earlier. He goes around humming all the time. He is smiling and in a really good mood. Don't get me wrong, I like working with him. He has always been nice and polite... just not as obviously happy as he has been the last few weeks."

"Really?" I was amazed.

"Yeah, it's like he is a completely new person. We already know he thinks very highly of you. And I do not mean in a business way. Anytime anyone mentions your name, he starts smiling and glowing. He's got it bad!"

I could feel the heat in my cheeks as I started to blush. "I think you and the rest of the department have an over-active imagination. We had a nice day but nothing extraordinary happened. I fell asleep on the couch. He fixed lunch. We played Scrabble. He hugged me before he left. That about sums it up." I was not ready to share Sam's singing to me or his kiss. Some things are too personal and meant to be treasured.

Linda eyed me suspiciously. "You're leaving something out. I can't believe you are holding out on me; and after I rescued the records from who knows what in Home Living yesterday!" she smiled accusingly.

"Seriously, Linda, we sat on the couch, he put his arms around me and I fell asleep on his shoulder. When I woke up, he was in the kitchen warming up leftover meatloaf to make sandwiches. He told me about Miss Martinez leaving and then we played Scrabble. He won the first game. I won the second one. We had just started playing a tiebreaker game when Dispatch called him and he had to leave. He hugged me goodbye. We had a nice, quiet day. I hated for him to go," I confessed.

"OK," she said doubtfully. "But be forewarned, I'm keeping my eye on you two!"

We both laughed. "So, are you ready to admit that you like him, too?" Linda asked with a gleam in her eye.

I smiled shyly. "I do like him; a lot. But I don't know."

"You don't know what?" she demanded in exasperation.

"Linda, I don't have a lot of experience with guys. In fact, almost none. In high school, I was everybody's friend; like a sister. Guys would come to me and ask how they could get this girl or that girl to go out with them. No one ever asked *me* out. I can count on one hand the dates I had in college. I just figured it was not meant for me to have that special someone. I do not want to read too much into what Sam does or says. I don't want to be disappointed when I realize it was all in my head."

"Well, I'm not trying to play with your emotions or give you false hope or anything like that. However, I can tell you, Reynolds is crazy about you. I would bet my badge on it," she replied seriously.

We were talking about the case when Linda exclaimed, "Well look who's here. Surprise, surprise! I told you," she nodded toward the buffet line.

I turned to see whom she was talking about. Sam, his plate piled high with slices of pizza, was walking toward our booth. "Mind if I join you or is this a ladies only meeting?" he smiled.

"Well it was…until you showed up. You might as well join us, we're through talking about you anyway," she teased. "How long did you drive around until you spotted my car?" she asked directly.

Sam slid into the booth beside me. "It wasn't hard, Chase. Everyone knows pizza is your food of choice," he laughed. He nudged me with his elbow. "How was your day?"

"Thankfully, rather normal," I answered. "What did you do today?"

"Chased rumors and dead end leads, mostly," he shook his head.

"Nothing new?" I concluded.

"No." His voice was a mixture of disappointment and frustration. "The Chief had me go over to Mable to check with Casey's Costume Shoppe there."

"Whatever for?" exclaimed Linda.

"Between my interview with Mrs. Perkins and the guys that talked with the kids from the other two schools, we figure Mr. X was wearing a fake beard and maybe a wig. Since they are the only store of that type anywhere close around here, he likely bought them there but they don't keep any kind of records that would show who bought what."

"What else did you find out from talking to Mrs. Perkins and the kids?" I asked.

"Mr. X is between five-ten and six feet; weighs around two hundred and fifteen pounds. He was sporting a shaggy brown beard. They really couldn't get a clear view of his face because of the hood he was wearing; one of the kids says they saw brown hair."

"Could be half the population of the county," observed Linda looking thoughtful.

"Right. Didn't exactly narrow it down very much," Sam agreed. "Would either of you ladies like something else from the buffet?" he inquired as he slid out of the booth.

"I'll take a slice of that cinnamon apple, if there's any left," Linda replied.

"No thanks. I'm good," I added.

"I told you he liked you," Linda whispered adamantly as soon as he was out of earshot.

"Would you stop?" I demanded in a quiet voice.

"Well, he did not pull up a chair and sit at the end of the booth. He did not sit with me. No…he went straight for your side and you know how he feels about sitting with his back to the door." She conveyed with a broad smile. I just shook my head.

Sam returned with two slices of cinnamon apple pizza for Linda and three slices of pepperoni for himself.

Chapter 21
Wednesday, March 8

Linda was at her usual place by the front door when Sam dropped me off at school. "Were your ears burning this morning?" she asked.

"What do you mean?" I responded as we walked to the room.

"You should have seen the looks on their faces when I told them about last night. Reynolds will probably get some ribbing today," she boasted.

"Linda! You've been gossiping about me and Sam?" I exclaimed.

"It's not gossip if it's true," she laughed merrily. "We're all happy for him. He deserves to have a great lady in his life," she added earnestly.

"Well, do you think you can stop thinking about me and Sam long enough to pay attention to the kids today?" I challenged light-heartedly.

"I can if you can," she shot back.

Linda was in the Blocks center building rockets with Ronnie and Dave while I was sitting on the floor in the Library center reading a book to Donna and Toni. Mrs. Post stepped in the door with a beautiful ivy plant in a wicker basket. Linda took it from her and started toward me, "This is a nice plant but he really should have sent flowers. They are much more romantic," she teased.

"Linda, that's not from Sam," I whispered with alarm. She stopped and looked at me with a puzzled expression. "Look at the bow." I told her.

She held it up and stared at the lime green ribbon adorning the front of the pot. She immediately set it down on the nearest bookshelf and retrieved the envelope that was tucked between the leaves. Removing the card, she read, "Glad you were brave enough to stay. Will this live longer than you?"

"Oh, that's it. How could I miss it?" I exclaimed as I jumped up from the floor. "Linda, I've got to go home." I grabbed my purse and dashed out of the room. Mrs. Post was almost back to the office when I rushed past her.

The Birthday Killer

"Mrs. Post, call Detective Reynolds and tell him to meet me at my apartment." I ran out the door and sprinted up the street. I was unlocking my door when I heard tires squealing around the corner. Sam burst in the door as I retrieved the poster from behind the table.

"Janet, oh Janet," he grabbed me and hugged me close. "I thought something happened to you! Thank God you're OK!" His voice quivered with emotion. I could feel his heart pounding.

"Sam, it's the flowers." I pulled away from him. "They all got the same flowers. Look." I pointed out the identical arrangements in the crime scene photos.

"How did you make that connection?" He shook his head; looking confused.

"He sent me a plant. Mr. X sent me a plant at school. And all of a sudden my mind just clicked. All the arrangements were the same. They are turned differently in the pictures and since they are not the main focus of the pictures, you really have to look at them to see they have the same flowers and they are put together the same way. Since the pictures are not in color, I did not make the connection before. I bet if you check, you'll find that the bows were lime green, too," I predicted.

"Can we sit down a minute?" Sam suggested. He put his hand to his temple, "I need to refocus just a bit." We sat at the table. Taking a deep breath to steady himself, he took my hand in both of his. "Where did the plant come from?" he asked.

"I don't know. I did not stop to check. Linda read the card to me and I ran out of the room."

"What did it say?"

"Glad you were brave enough to stay. Will this live longer than you?"

"Let's go back to school so I can get it. I need to check and see if Mrs. Layne got one, too." Sam's mind had shifted back into work mode.

On the way to school, Sam used his police radio to confirm that Mrs. Layne had also received a plant; Lakin Florist had been the source. Linda looked relieved when we walked in. "What was all of that about?" she queried. "You scared me to death tearing out of here like that!"

"I'm sorry, Linda. When I looked at the plant, suddenly all the pictures of the flower arrangements at the crime scenes flashed through my mind and somehow it just clicked that each one of the victims had gotten the same flower arrangements. They were more in the background of the crime scene photos so I suppose I hadn't really focused on them. I never put it together. I guess I kind of freaked out. I just knew I had to show Sam. I thought it might be important."

"Well, it is a clue that we all had missed," agreed Sam. "And one that might just be the one we needed to break the case. But I have to say Chase is right; you gave us both a scare!"

I hung my head. "I really am sorry. Something inside me just exploded and I reacted. I didn't mean to scare anybody." I said apologetically.

Sam put his arms around me. "All is forgiven."

"Don't give her any more ammunition," I nodded toward Linda who was eagerly taking it all in.

"I know. I've already heard about her reports this morning." He raised an eyebrow at her.

Randy stomped up to us, grabbed my hand and scowled at Sam, "MY Carter!"

"Got a little competition there, Reynolds. You better watch out," Linda laughed.

"Thought I was avoiding that by putting you in here. Didn't realize it would be an inside threat." Sam volleyed back at her.

"OK you guys. I am feeling a little uncomfortable here. You," I looked at Sam, "go check out the florist. Miss Linda, go listen to records with Ronnie. Come on Randy, let's go draw a picture," I directed as I led Randy to the Art center.

Sam and Linda started laughing. "I'll pick you up after school," he said to me as he walked out the door. "See you later," he directed authoritatively at Linda.

The information Sam was able to get from the florist was not the case breaker we had hoped for, but it did shed some light on the situation. Sam shared his findings as we ate supper. The clerk remembered Mr. X coming in to pick up the flowers because his appearance seem rather strange to her and he always paid cash. She recalled he had worn the same grey sweat suit with the hood pulled up over his head and that his bushy brown beard did not look real. She had not really thought much about the second time he came in but on his third trip to make the identical purchase, she had asked him why he was getting the same thing every month. He told her they were his wife's favorite kind and he was trying to stay on her good side. Since the flowers had never been mentioned in the newspaper she did not make any kind of connection.

"We don't even know if Mr. X is really married. That was probably just part of his cover up. I'm not even sure if it makes any difference." Sam summed up his visit to the florist as he took another bite of the Beef Stew and cornbread I had made for supper. "The order for the plants for you and

Mrs. Layne came in the mail with the cards and enough cash to cover their cost. It was postmarked in Lakin. Not much to go on." He sighed in frustration.

Chapter 22
Thursday, March 9

Thursday morning started with a bang, literally. At two eighteen in the morning, the transformer at the end of the block blew out with a loud boom and plunged the whole area into darkness. I sat straight up in bed startled awake by the offending noise. Molly yelped and jumped up on the bed. I held her close and tried to offer some reassurance. There was dead silence and pitch-blackness; it took me a few minutes to figure out what had happened. I felt around in the drawer of the bedside table and found my flashlight. Then I went to the closet and got my travel alarm out of my suitcase. I wound it up, checked my watch and set the small clock to the correct time. I would still have to get up for school, electricity or not.

About half an hour later work trucks started gathering at the corner to replace the busted transformer. With warning lights flashing, vehicles beeping as they jockeyed into position and the indistinguishable voices of the workmen calling out directions, I gave up on trying to go back to sleep. I lay there thinking about Sam and the events that had brought us together when I noticed a movement at the bedroom window. I sat up and watched as the shadow of someone moving outside on the walkway was illuminated by the floodlights the workers had set up so they could see. They walked past my window only to return and stop a moment later. My heart pounded, my breathing became rapid and shallow as paralyzing fear seized my body.

I forced my legs to move as I got out of bed, donned my robe, crept into the living room, and dialed Sam's number. I clutched the receiver with both hands. He answered on the second ring. "Hello?" came his groggy greeting, "This is Reynolds."

"Sam, there is someone outside my bedroom window," I choked out in a panicky whisper.

"I'm on my way." His voice was instantly clear and alert. "Go lock yourself in the bathroom," he instructed. I heard the click as he hung up and then overwhelming nothingness on the other end. I stood rooted to the spot feeling as if my lifeline had just been cut. I had never felt so alone. Molly nudged my leg and I snapped back to reality.

I hurriedly gathered the blanket from the foot of my bed and retreated into the bathroom. Molly shadowed my every step. I wrapped up in the blanket and sat on the floor; my back against the door. Molly climbed into my lap; her little body trembling. I wasn't sure if she was scared or cold from the lack of heat in the apartment. The tears started flowing. "Oh Heavenly Father, please keep us safe." I prayed earnestly. "Help Sam …to get here… fast." I pleaded between sobs. I could hear the droning of the machinery and heavy equipment as the workers endeavored to switch out the transformer.

My body tensed to attention when I heard men's voices coming from outside my apartment. I couldn't make out what they were saying but I could tell it was more than two different people talking. After what seemed like an eternity, I heard Sam knocking on my door and calling my name. I flew out of the bathroom and flung open the front door. I threw myself into his arms; tears streaming down my face. "It's OK, Janet. It's OK," he soothed. "Let's go sit on the couch," he managed to maneuver me back inside the apartment. "You're safe. Everything is OK." He stroked my hair and gently rocked me back and forth.

"Oh Sam, I was so scared." I cried into his shoulder.

"I know, baby, I know." He continued to speak quietly. "I'm here now. Everything is going to be OK."

"It's over; it's finally over." I exclaimed through my waning tears.

Sam groaned. "I wish I could tell you that it is, but it's not. That wasn't him."

"What?" I drew away from him; searching his face in confusion. "What do you mean it wasn't him?"

"It was your apartment manager. He was just up here trying to get a better view of what was going on at the corner."

"No, no, no…please tell me it's over!" I begged hysterically. "I can't… do this… anymore, Sam." My tears returned with tormented fury; my body racked with agonizing sobs. Sliding to the floor, I pulled my knees up to my chest; wrapped my arms around them and started rocking in distress.

"I'm so sorry, Janet." He dropped to the floor beside me. He embraced me gently, his arms forming a wall of protection around me. "My precious Janet, I wish I could take away your pain." His voice was full of anguish as he placed a lingering kiss on my forehead.

W. Kay Lynn

Slowly, in the comforting shelter of his arms, I relaxed; my tears subsided. I realized Sam was humming and I began to feel a peace seeping into my heart as I thought about the words of the song.

"Sam?"

"Yes, dear."

"Will you sing it for me?"

His voice sounded clear and comforting in the darkness. I stretched out my legs and leaned against him.

"When my sky is clear and bright,
When I find it dark as night;
Just to trust and do the right,
That's enough for me.
That's enough for me, that's enough for me;
Just to trust and do the right, that's enough for me.

When my heart is filled with joy,
When the foe would fain destroy,
If I'm in the Lord's employ,
That's enough for me.
That's enough for me, that's enough for me;
If I'm in the Lord's employ, that's enough for me.

When I'm pressed with toil and care,
When the cross seems hard to bear,
Just the grace of God to share,
That's enough for me.
That's enough for me, that's enough for me;
Just the grace of God to share, that's enough for me.

When I part with loved ones here,
When I'm tempted death to fear,
Just to know my Lord is near,
That's enough for me.
That's enough for me, that's enough for me;
Just to know my Lord is near, that's enough for me."[4]

"Thank you, Sam." I sighed contentedly.

"Any time," he promised.

---

[4] "That's Enough For Me", William J. Henry, Public Domain

Chapter 23
Thursday, March 9

I jumped when the alarm went off at six o'clock; its metallic clanging shattering the calm that had finally settled into the apartment. "I'll get it," Sam offered.

"I wish we didn't have to move. What if I just call in this morning and don't go to school," I suggested.

Sam stood and offered a hand to help me up. "Sit on the couch and we can discuss it when I come back." He returned in an instant after silencing the offending timepiece. "Your clock is flashing. The electricity is back on. I thought I noticed the noise winding down at the corner." As if on cue, the electric wall heater clicked on. "We can sit here until things warm up a bit."

"Do you want to share my blanket?" I asked.

"No, I'm OK. Thanks." He sat beside me. "Now, about you staying home today…certainly you can do what you want to do but I can't stay here with you. Probably, since the electricity is back on, I should be leaving pretty soon."

"Why?"

"Because Jackson was up here when I got here this morning talking to the apartment manager and he knows I am still here."

"Who's Jackson?" I interrupted.

"Your overnight undercover agent. He spotted someone up here by your apartment and he came to check it out." Sam informed me stiffly. "I have no doubt that Chase will hear about all of this and you know how she is…" He paused. "Who knows what the story will be when she gets through with all her embellishments."

"You're right, it could get really embarrassing!" I concurred with a smile. "Thank you, Sam, for coming. I couldn't have gotten through this without you."

"I'm glad you called me. That's what I am here for… to make sure you feel safe." His posture was rigid and he sounded official and a little distant.

"Well," I stood up feeling as if I was the biggest idiot in the world. "I guess I better start getting ready and you need to get on with your day. Thank you again. I suppose I will see you later." I hoped my disappointment didn't show.

Sam left and I went to sit on my bed. Molly climbed up in my lap. "Oh Molly, I feel so stupid. Apparently, I let my imagination run away with me, again, and read more into our relationship than what is really there. I should not have listened to Linda. I know better. He acted so formal. And did you hear the way he said he was here to make me 'feel safe'? I *am* just a job to him… like 'other duties as assigned'." Molly listened devotedly while I poured out my heart. "I really like him Molly. He makes me feel special but I guess I had better stop those thoughts! I'm glad I realized it before I made a bigger fool of myself than I already have."

Linda, as usual, met me at the front door of the school. "I hear you have a wayward squirrel blowing out the transformer to thank for some private time with Reynolds."

"News travels fast." I responded glumly.

"So, what happened?" She inquired. "Tell me all about it!"

"Nothing." I answered dully.

"Oh, come on. I know he was there for a couple of hours," she pressed.

"I saw someone outside my window. I panicked and called Sam. He came over and we sat in the living room and talked until the lights came back on. End of story."

"Jackson said you were really glad to see him!" she prodded for more information.

"Yes. When he got there, I latched on to him like a crazy woman. I was scared. He calmed me down. I am sorry there is not more to tell but that is all there is. He is not interested in me that way. He as much as said out right that I was just his job for the moment. Hopefully in a week or two, things will be back to normal and he can get on with his life and I can get on with mine." I summarized dejectedly.

"He said that?" she asked doubtingly.

"Not in those exact words but, yes, that is what he said." I could see by the look on her face that she was not accepting my explanation. "I would prefer to change the subject."

"I'm sorry, Janet." She spoke sympathetically. "I can't believe he's not in love with you. I've seen the way he looks…"

"Linda, please; just drop it." I pleaded. "I have a class to teach and that needs to be my focus; not chasing some silly school-girl dream that isn't there."

Despite my best intentions, my mind kept wandering back to Sam. The feel of his strong arms around me. The sound of his voice soothing and comforting. The beauty of his singing. The way he made me laugh.

"Oh, my Carter," Randy patted me on the back looking concerned, "not cry." I did not realize there were tears rolling down my cheeks.

"Thank you Randy, I'm OK." I told him. "At least I know your devotion is true." I smiled at him as I wiped the moisture off my face.

Linda and I talked quietly during rest time. "It's fine with me if you want to leave early," she offered. "You look worn out."

"I am *definitely* tired. I don't function so well when I don't get any sleep." I admitted. "But, I'm OK. I can make it until the end of the day. But I guarantee you this; I *will* be in bed shortly after I get home and get Molly situated."

The afternoon crawled by. I almost wished I had taken Linda up on her offer and gone home early. I left as soon as the kids were gone. Molly seemed to be a little less jubilant when I got home. "Are you as tired as I am girlfriend?" I asked her. She wagged her tail and stood by the door waiting for me to take her out. As we approached the corner of the building, Sam drove up.

"Mind if I join you?"

"If you want to," I responded dully. We walked around to the lot and I let Molly run free. She trotted around in her usual pattern, smelling and checking out different spots.

I sat down on the bench, folding my arms in front of me. Sam sat beside me. My heart ached at his closeness. "I thought I would see if you wanted to go get some tacos," he invited.

"No, thank you." I replied. "I'm tired. I'm going to bed as soon as we get back upstairs."

"Are you sure? You have to eat something," he encouraged.

"I'm not hungry. But thanks anyway." Molly came up wagging her tail at Sam. "See you later," I stood up quickly.

"Janet," Sam reached out and took my hand. "What's wrong?" I fought back the tears that wanted to flow and withdrew my hand from his.

"Nothing, Sam. I am just tired. Talk to you tomorrow." I walked back to the apartment without looking back. I heard Sam getting in his car. I felt him watching me all the way to my door.

As much as I longed for it, sleep did not come. I lay there, my mind racing. I thought about Sam. I thought about my class. I thought about Mr. X. I thought about the evidence poster. I wondered how Mrs. Layne was handling our situation. I envied Miss Martinez being home and safe without having to worry about the events taking place. Finally, sometime after midnight, exhaustion overtook me and I drifted off to sleep.

When the alarm went off at six o'clock, I decided I was not going to school. I needed time to rest and regroup. I made all the necessary calls to have my class covered; Mrs. Taylor agreed to sub and Mr. Brewer was very understanding and concurred that a "mental health day" might be just what I needed. After taking Molly outside, I went back to bed. A little after nine the telephone rang. I jumped up and hurried into the living room to answer it.

"Hello," I answered.

"Janet, is everything all right?" It was Sam. "Jackson said you didn't go in to school today."

"Yeah, Sam. I am fine. I just needed some thinking time and a little more sleep than I have been getting these last few days." I responded. "Oh," I added. "I wanted to apologize for calling you out in the middle of the night. I forgot that the undercover guy was on duty. I'm sorry I bothered you."

"It wasn't a bother. Of course I want you to call me." He sounded confused by my statement. "How about if I bring some burgers over for lunch?" He suggested.

"No, that's OK. I will pass this time. Thanks anyway. Hey, I need to take Molly out so I had better go. Thanks for calling." I hung up the phone before I started crying. It hurt to talk to him.

I put on some old clothes and headed to the kitchen. I cleaned out the refrigerator, washed the empty containers, and took out the trash. I had just finished sweeping and mopping the floor when someone knocked on the door. Molly barked excitedly and started jumping up and down.

I was seriously considering not opening the door when Sam called out. "Janet. It's me."

My heart fluttered. "I'm sorry Sam, I'm not dressed." I lied.

"Reed said you took out your trash a little while ago."

"Yes, I did but I went back to bed." I rolled my eyes; I had not thought about somebody seeing me.

"Janet, is everything OK?"

The Birthday Killer

"Yes, Sam. I am fine. Go back to work. I'm sure Jackson or Reed or whoever it is will let you know if I need something." I willed him to go.

"I'll call you later." His voice was full of uncertainty and disappointment.

"OK. Bye" I heard him walking away. Molly sat down and looked up at me with a puzzled expression. I picked her up and carried her over to the couch. "I'm sorry girl. It is just too hard to be around him right now. I am so stupid." I berated myself. "I don't know why I thought he would have feelings for me. I mean, it's only been three weeks! I do not even know the man... and yet... I feel like I have known him my whole life." Molly licked my chin. I buried my face in her neck and cried.

After lunch, I was restless, full of nervous energy. I changed the sheets on my bed, straightened the dresser drawers, rearranged the closet, vacuumed, dusted, cleaned the oven and scrubbed the bathtub. I even thought about cleaning the windows but I figured Reed would tell Sam. I retrieved the calendar from the kitchen wall and sat down at the table. I looked at the poster we used to record the crime scene information for a few minutes and started writing the names of the victims on the dates of the murders onto the calendar. The telephone rang. I looked at the clock, five twenty. I knew it was Sam so I elected not to answer. He waited fifteen minutes before calling again. "I can't talk to you Sam," I said to the ringing instrument. "I'm just not up to it right now." Another ten minutes passed and he called again.

Twenty minutes later, I heard footsteps followed by a knock on the door. "Janet, open the door. Please." His voice sounded concerned.

I opened the door about half way and an excited Molly lunged for Sam. I picked her up. "I'm sorry Sam. Please go. I just need to be alone right now." I explained. The pained expression on his face pierced my heart.

"Have I done something to upset you?" he questioned.

"No, Sam. It is not you. It's me. I'll see you later." I closed the door. He stood on the other side of the door for several minutes before he finally retreated.

Chapter 24
Saturday, March 11

I awoke Saturday morning at seven fifteen. I was a little surprised that Molly had not wanted to go out before then. However, I figured she had been as disturbed by my tossing and turning all night as much as I had been. I decided since I was awake anyway, I would get an early start on the chores for the day, and hopefully beat everyone else to the apartment laundry room. I put all the dirty clothes in a basket; got the detergent, fabric softener, Molly, her leash, and her ball and headed downstairs. I started everything washing and took Molly around to the back lot. I sat there watching her running and playing with the shadows as they danced through the branches of the Redbud trees heavy with bright pink blossoms. Several times when I threw her ball, she caught it in mid-air. After plenty of time for the washing machines to be finished, we returned to the laundry room to put the clothes in the dryer. With that task completed, we headed upstairs.

We had been back in the apartment less than five minutes when there was a loud knocking on the door. I was glad I had remembered to latch the safety chain.

I opened it to find Sam standing there with a box of donuts in one hand and a bouquet of yellow Tulips in the other.

"What are you doing here?" I exclaimed with surprise.

"Janet, we've got to talk! Can I come in?" He insisted urgently.

I unhooked the safety chain and stepped aside so he could enter. He set the donuts on the table, turned and handed the flowers to me.

"What are you doing?" I asked in confusion.

"I am not about to lose the best thing that ever happened to me because of some stupid remark I made." His voice was solemn and his gaze was intense. He took the flowers from me, laid them on the table, reached out for my hands and pulled me toward him. He slid his hands up my arms to my shoulders. "Thursday morning before the alarm went off and we were sitting in front of the couch; you had finally relaxed enough to doze off. I felt the tenseness leaving your body and I realized you *trusted* me and… I hoped… needed me. I was suddenly aware just how much I care about you and… it scared me. And then when I went in your room to turn off the alarm and realized that the electricity was back on I could only think of how it might look for me to have been here all night. I did not want to give anyone cause to think less of you. Moreover, for the record, you are not, nor have you ever been 'just a job' to me. I am so sorry if I made you think that."

"You've been talking to Linda," I accused.

"Yes, and I'm glad I did," came his quick reply. "Janet, I was attracted to you from the first moment I saw you. I was here yesterday morning because I *wanted* to be here. I want to *always* be here; to protect you, to hold you, to comfort you."

"You're not just saying that? I know I am a bother. I am always in a panic. I…"

He silenced me with a warm and tender kiss. My heart started to sing. I leaned against him, his arms holding me tightly.

"I don't know what to say," I shook my head.

"You don't have to say anything. Just forgive me for pushing you away; that was totally the opposite of what I wanted to do." He smiled. He was quiet for a moment and then with a twinkle in his eye he asked, "Do you have any coffee to go with the donuts?"

"Why did you bring donuts? Haven't you already eaten?"

"Yesterday you said you didn't want burgers. And I figured it was too early for lunch anyway."

"I didn't want *you*." I responded. "It hurt too much to talk to you; to be around you."

Sam groaned. "I am so sorry."

"Apology accepted. It will just take a few minutes to make some coffee." I headed toward the kitchen.

Sam turned to follow me but stopped at the table. "What are you doing with this?" he inquired looking at the wall calendar and the case information poster.

"Marking the dates of the murders. I was hoping if I could visualize it in a different format maybe something would make sense."

"Did it?"

"Not yet. I was kind of interrupted in the middle of it." I smiled. "I believe that was about the time the telephone started ringing…and ringing."

"I was worried about you. Didn't mean to be a pest but I could not understand what happened for you to be so stand-offish. Didn't sleep much last night; kept going over the last few days, wracking my brain to figure it out. Then this morning I decided to talk to Chase and see if she had any clue."

I set cups and napkins on the table and we sat down to wait for the coffee to finish brewing. Sam picked up the calendar and scanned the pages. "At least we know more now than we did when we first put all of this together." He observed. "Just wished we had all the answers."

I returned to the kitchen to get the coffee pot and a vase for the flowers. Sam poured the coffee while I put the flowers in the vase. "Thanks for the flowers, Sam. They're really pretty."

"I was hoping they would get me in the door." He smiled sincerely. He munched thoughtfully on a chocolate covered donut. "Hey, do you have anything going on this afternoon? Would you be interested in going to the park? We could take Molly and she could have a new place to explore. What do you say?" He asked brightly.

"That might be fun. And to tell the truth, I really would not mind getting out of the apartment for a while. I just need to get my clothes out of the dryer downstairs. They should be finished by now."

"Great!" he beamed. "I'll help you get your clothes and then we can head out."

I reached in the dryer, got several handfuls of warm clothes, and put them in the basket. The last thing I pulled out was the sheets that had become a big wad all rolled up together. I shook them apart and a lime green towel fell out from between them. I recoiled in horror. "That's not mine, Sam. That's not mine!"

"I think it would be mine." A young college boy walked in the door. "I noticed it wasn't in my basket when I was folding the towels. I came to see if I left it in the dryer."

I just stared at him, unable to move. Sam picked up the towel and turned back to me. "Janet, if we have everything why don't you take the basket back upstairs. I'll be there in just a minute." He directed pointedly while looking intently into my eyes.

Dutifully, I hurried back to the apartment. I sat down on the couch and put the basket of clothes on the floor in front of me. I started shaking and my breathing became labored. Molly jumped up on the couch beside me and whined. All I could see was the lime green towel falling out of the sheets.

Sam returned a few minutes later and headed straight for the telephone. He turned to me and held out his hand. I went to stand beside him and he put one arm around me and pulled me close. "Gerber, this is Reynolds. I need you to run a check on a nineteen year old, white male, freshman at the junior college. The name is Jeffery Grant. I need everything you can get on him. Correct. Is Hicks on duty? Yeah, send him. OK, I'll check back with you later." He hung up the telephone and put his other arm around me.

"Oh, Sam, he lives here. Mr. X lives *here*! Can't you have him arrested?" I exclaimed hysterically.

"We don't know that for sure. But I will definitely find out one way or the other." He reasoned with me. "Janet, we can't arrest a man for having a lime green towel." Sam hugged me tightly. "Do we need to sit down?" he asked gently.

"No, I'm OK as long as you are with me. Let's just go. I want to get away from here."

Chapter 25
Saturday, March 11

Lakin Community Park, Sam explained as we drove, "is the culmination of over seven years of planning, fund raising, and citizen involvement. The land, almost a hundred acres, was donated by Emily Lakin, the widow of a once prominent businessman whose family was instrumental in establishing Lakin back in the 1800's. There were committees formed for every aspect of the project; almost everybody in town was involved in one way or another. They ended up with a really nice place for people to enjoy. It's been open about six years." We stopped at the Chicken Shack on the way to the park and picked up food for a picnic lunch.

The park proved to be a very impressive site. A three-foot high red brick wall topped with a four-foot chain link fence marked the border around the entire park. The entrance was framed by two ten foot red brick pillars connected at the top with black wrought letters and scroll-work proclaiming "LAKIN COMMUNITY PARK   EST. 1966." The parking lot just inside the entrance was large enough for about a hundred cars. It was surrounded by Pecan trees and flowerbeds bursting with yellow Daffodils, blue and purple Crocus, purple and yellow Pansies, and white Snowdrops with breaks in the flowerbeds where the pavement marked the entrances to the three sections of the park. The area to the right hosted four tennis courts, two basketball courts and a baseball field. There were small bleachers positioned strategically throughout for fans to sit and watch the action.

The center section directly across from the main entrance was the garden area that had two designated places; a memorial rose garden and a community vegetable garden. Apparently, Mrs. Lakin was a lover of roses. There were over two hundred different rose bushes arranged in various beds separated by a three-foot wide brick path that meandered among them. The center of the rose garden accommodated a small goldfish pond with a bust of Mrs. Lakin set on a granite stand with a bronze plaque attached that related her legacy positioned nearby. Stone benches were advantageously placed throughout for visitors to relax and enjoy their surroundings. The community garden spot was a large plot that was available for anyone to plant and grow produce during the growing seasons. According to Sam, fifth Grade classes from the local schools rotated field trips during the spring to plant and take care of an assortment of vegetables for anyone in town to come and harvest.

"You mean anyone can come pick vegetables? Even if they didn't plant them?" I asked in disbelief.

"Well, theoretically, yes. But there is sort of an unwritten code of ethics that if you come to get produce from the garden you will help out by weeding or watering, etc." he clarified.

The area to the left of the parking lot had three basic sections. The first section hosted a dozen cement picnic tables with benches spaced out over a wide area; each protected with a blue, green or red tin roof covering. Beside each was a small steel firebox with a grate across the top of it, mounted on a cement pedestal for cooking hotdogs or burgers and such. Beyond the tables was a playground section featuring swings, slides, teeter totters, spring mounted rocking animals, monkey bars, a merry-go-round, and a sand box. The far section was a fair sized grove of assorted trees and bushes with hiking trails cut through the underbrush. Sam pointed out the six foot wide "walking track" around the perimeter of this entire area of the park just inside the brick and chain link fence. "Once around is a mile," He informed me.

After Sam had given me the grand tour, we selected a blue roofed picnic table and set out our chicken dinner. The weather was cool but pleasant and there were quite a few families and small groups of people using the different areas of the park. Sam said grace and we helped ourselves to the chicken, potatoes, and corn on the cob. I picked off some of the meat for Molly who danced around excitedly at the special treat. Sam had even thought about Molly when he ordered something for us to drink. She had her own cup of water while we drank lemonade.

"This is a really nice place!" I decided with admiration. "Who takes care of all of this? It's obviously well maintained."

"Along with the land, Mrs. Lakin set up a fund that would provide for a caretaker," Sam shared. "The city provides the workers and uses the funds for repairs and on-going maintenance."

Two young boys from my school approached our table. "Hi, Miss Carter, can we play with your dog?" I recognized Jack and Toby from the second grade class across the hall from my room.

"Sure, just keep her in sight." I admonished. "Here's her ball. She *loves* to play fetch." They took off running past the swings with Molly in hot pursuit.

Sam reached across the table for my hand. "Janet, I want to tell you something. Do you remember that first day when we met in Brewer's office?"

"Yes." I nodded.

"You will probably think I am crazy, but when we shook hands…" he paused and took a deep breath. He looked at me with a seriousness I had not seen before.

"Yes?" I urged.

"When we shook hands, God…" he paused again. "God told me… 'here's the woman I have for you'. It stunned me; sort of threw me for a loop. It took me a few minutes to regain my composure."

I searched his eyes. I thought back to our first encounter. I knew he was being completely honest with me. "Why are you telling me this now?" I wondered aloud.

"Because I truly believe that we are meant to be together. God would not bring you into my life to let you be taken away. Maybe knowing that will help you get through all of this a little easier. I know it does not make it go away or make it any less dangerous for you. But maybe it's at least a positive thought for you to hold on to." he said quietly.

"Thank you, Sam." We sat in a comfortable silence for several minutes.

"I guess we should be heading back." He said with resignation. Maybe we can stop at the Dairy Bar and get some ice cream on the way home." Sam started gathering up our trash and I went to get Molly. I scanned the playground for the boys and spotted them playing on the merry-go-round. Molly was nowhere in sight.

I rushed up to them. "Where's Molly?" I demanded.

"That man took her." Toby said innocently.

"He said you told him to get her," added Jack.

"Sam," I yelled. "He's got Molly!"

"Where did he go?" Sam came sprinting over.

"That way." They pointed toward the hiking trails. I started running.

"Janet! Wait!" commanded Sam. I stopped. He turned back to the boys. "What did the man look like?" he quizzed.

"I don't know," shrugged Jack.

"What color was he wearing?" Sam prodded.

"I think it was gray," Toby replied hesitantly.

"Yeah," agreed Jack, "and he had brown hair all over his face." He recalled.

"Thanks boys." Sam patted them on the head. We started running toward the trees. "Let's start on that side," he pointed toward the right.

As soon as we reached the edge of the trees, I started calling for her. There was no response. Just inside the tree line the trail forked. "I'll go this way and you can look on that path," I suggested.

"No, ma'am," Sam disagreed firmly. "We stay together. It might take a little longer but I'm not letting you go anywhere by yourself right now." I kept calling her name and still no response.

"Oh Sam," I cried frantically, tears streaming down my face. "What if he's done something terrible to her?"

"Listen!" Sam stopped and put up his hand. "Molly!" he called. I heard a pitiful whimper. "This way," Sam directed as he started back the way we had just come. "Molly!" he called again. The muted whine was closer.

"Miss Carter! Miss Carter! There he goes!" I heard Jack and Toby calling from the edge of the trees. "That man is running away!"

Sam grabbed my shoulders. "You stay right here!" He raced down the trail and out of sight. I turned my attention back to finding Molly.

"Hey girl," I called following the sound of her muffled yelps. I rounded a curve in the trail and there she was, standing in the middle of the path tied to a tree with a green rope. It was wrapped firmly around her snout like a muzzle, looped around her neck and then tightly knotted around the bottom branch of a Redbud tree. I ran to her and gathered her into my arms. "Oh, Molly," I hugged her close. "Thank God you're OK. Let me see if I can get you undone." I tried loosening the knots but my hands were shaking so badly I could not get a good grip on them.

"Janet," Sam called from a distance.

"I found her." I called back between sobs. "We're over here,"

Sam appeared around the curve. "Hey girl, let's get this off of you," he said gently as he pulled his pocketknife out of his pocket, knelt down beside us and started cutting the ropes that bound her.

"I guess you didn't catch him." I surmised.

"No. He was already by the picnic tables when I cleared the trees. By the time I got to the parking lot he was gone. And of course, there wasn't anyone else in the parking lot that could have identified his vehicle."

As soon as she was unrestrained, Molly started jumping and barking. Sam caught her in the middle of one of her jumps; she licked his face enthusiastically. "I would say she is glad to be free." I noted. "Oh Sam, I don't know what I would do without you and Molly." I added reflectively trying to stifle my weeping.

"I pray we never have to find out." Sam commented seriously, as he set her down and put his arm around my shoulders. I cried all the way back to the car. After we were settled in, Sam put his arms around me; Molly sat shaking between us. "You know he could have hurt her if he wanted to, but I don't think that's his plan. He just wants to scare you as much as he can. He is playing with you," he added angrily. I felt his muscles tense momentarily.

"Well, he's doing a great job of that!" I declared; my tears flowing. "I just want to go home and hide. I can't go anywhere without being afraid he is going to show up!"

"I know." He whispered lovingly. "That's why I'm not letting you go anywhere without me." He placed a tender kiss on my temple. Molly finally settled down and fell asleep; her head on Sam's lap. I laid my head on his shoulder.

"Oh Sam," I sighed. "God must love me a whole lot to put someone as wonderful as you in my life." His arms gave me a little squeeze. We sat in the parking lot until it was almost dark; not saying anything, just enjoying the quiet closeness.

Chapter 26
Sunday, March 12

Mrs. Layne approached me when we walked into the Sunday school room. "I wanted to see if you had any plans for lunch. I thought maybe you and Detective Reynolds could join us at Potter's Cafeteria." She invited.

"I can't speak for Sam, but I would love to. I really would like a chance to just sit and talk to you." I accepted.

Sam came up behind me. "Now, you know if you are talking about food, I am always in! They have a really good buffet," he commented.

"You would know." I affirmed with a chuckle; nudging his arm with my elbow.

Pastor Jenkins reminded everyone that the "Spring Fling" the church hosted every year at the end of the Spring Break session for the local schools and Junior College was set for two weeks from yesterday. "We still need volunteers to sort through the yard sale items and get everything priced. In addition, of course, we need more cakes for the cakewalk. You can sign up for the places we still have needs on the paper in the foyer," he informed us.

Sam leaned over and whispered, "What are you going to sign up for?"

"*WE* can check the list after church," I countered.

We met the Layne's at Potter's after church and went through the serving line together. Our trays loaded with savory choices, we wandered through the dining room until we found an extra-large corner booth that had just been vacated. We waited while the busboy cleaned off the table then Sam and I scooted in first toward the middle. Mrs. Layne sat beside me with Ashley on the outside on her right. Mr. Layne sat by Sam with Mark, Junior on the outside on his left.

Half way through the meal, the men tired of small talk and started discussing sports. "What do you think of that new baseball team they're bringing in from Washington, D.C.? I think they are going to call them the

'Texas Rangers.' From what I've heard; they aren't that good of a team." Mr. Layne began the conversation.

Mrs. Layne and I looked at each other and shook our heads. "I'm not into sports," I admitted. "How are you doing?" I asked quietly. "Are you able to put any of this out of your mind?"

"Not really. My goal is to just get through each day the best I can." She responded. "I hate the feeling that he's watching me all the time. Like right now, I just know that he is here spying on us. I know it sounds crazy but I can't help myself."

"I know what you mean; I find it dreadfully intimidating. I know that *most* of the time he is not around but he *was* yesterday. He followed us out to the park and even took my dog and tied her to a tree." I shared.

"How did he do that?" she asked in alarm.

"Two second graders from my school had asked if they could play with Molly while Sam and I were sitting at a picnic table talking. Mr. X told them that I said he could take her. Then he took her into the hiking trails and tied her up." My voice trembled with emotion as I told the story. Sam reached over and took my hand giving it a slight squeeze.

"That *is* scary! I don't think he has been that close to me, yet. However, I do think he has been calling the house. If I answer the telephone, I can hear breathing but they don't say anything. If Mark answers, they just hang up real fast. Needless to say, I've stopped answering the telephone."

"Good plan. I have not had that happen yet and I hope it does not start! Have you heard anything from Miss Martinez?"

"No. I was thinking about her yesterday," replied Mrs. Layne.

Mr. Layne excused himself to take Mark, Junior to the rest room. "Sam," I asked, "Has anybody heard from Miss Martinez?"

"Yes, her contact actually talked to her Friday. She is doing fine. Relieved that her birthday is past and she is still alive." He relayed.

"Is she coming back?" Mrs. Layne wanted to know.

"Not until we catch him."

"It's a good thing Mr. Nicholas guaranteed her job. If she even *wants* to come back; after all of this." I noted.

"If it weren't for Mark and the kids, I probably would have done exactly what she did…get the heck out of Dodge!" exclaimed Mrs. Layne.

Mr. Layne returned with Mark, Junior, "Look who we found eating all by himself. I insisted he come join us." Mr. Nicholas, looking a little uncomfortable, carrying his tray of food accompanied him. He pulled up a chair and sat at the open end of the booth.

"I feel like I am just barging in," he apologized.

"No, it's fine," greeted Sam. "We're just discussing sports and how much better we could do if we were the coach." The men laughed. "How much longer do you think Staubach will be playing?" And with that, the men's conversation changed to football and the Dallas Cowboys.

"You teach a fairly broad age group, don't you? How does that work?" inquired Mrs. Layne.

"I really do more grouping by ability than by age. And I cover everything from 'What color is that?' to 'What do you think the character in the story meant when they said that?' We use a lot of manipulatives and sing a lot of action songs when we are learning new concepts." I explained. "I wouldn't know what to do with a room full of fifth graders." I admitted. "How do you do that?" I questioned.

"It's not too bad. I just follow the curriculum the district set up for us. I have a system for good behavior and most of the kids are great. I really only have two students that I have to keep my thumb on." She replied. "I am so looking forward to Spring Break. It's hard to believe that it is just a week away."

"I forgot all about it until the Pastor mentioned it this morning." I admitted.

"I can tell you haven't been teaching very long," She laughed.

The two Layne children were getting restless so we decided to disburse to our respective homes. Mr. Nicholas thanked us for letting him join the group. "You ladies have a good week," he nodded. "I just signed your card," he looked at me.

"Excuse me?" I asked in confusion.

"Oh, the District sends out cards every month for special occasions. My secretary brings me a pile of cards every Friday to sign for the next week. Yours was in the stack," he explained hurriedly.

"How nice," I replied flatly. I was surprised by my feeling of displeasure. Suddenly I realized that I did not want anyone to know when my birthday was. It had become a terrifying event that even I did not want to acknowledge myself.

"And I guess I will be meeting with you in the morning," he addressed Sam.

"Yep, same time, same place," nodded Sam in affirmation.

Walking to the car Sam put his arm around my shoulders. "Are you OK? You seem a little tense." He observed.

"Mr. Nicholas just reminded me what I have been trying to ignore. My birthday is three days away and I am not even sure I will live to see the end of the week. I'm scared, Sam." My voice broke as I started to cry.

W. Kay Lynn

"Oh, Janet," Sam stopped in the middle of the parking lot and wrapped his arms around me. I cried into his shoulder. He led me to the car and once we were seated, he put his arms around me again. "I cannot even begin to imagine how truly difficult this is for you. But I believe with all my heart that everything will be OK."

"I believe God will protect me, too. But Sam, you know as well as I do, bad things still happen to people who don't deserve it." His arms tightened around me and I relished in the feel of his strength. "I wish this moment, right now would never end. Please don't let go; just hold me." I begged.

Sam kissed my cheek and whispered in my ear, "I'm here as long as you want me. I am not going anywhere."

After a little while, when a feeling of peace and security had filled my being, I was ready to go home. "I guess we need to go. Molly will be wondering if I am coming to let her out."

As we drove to my apartment, Sam reached over and took my hand. "Did you have a good visit with Mrs. Layne?"

"Yes. It helps to know that we are both dealing with the same struggles. It makes me feel a little better about myself knowing that I'm not necessarily overreacting like a crazy person to everything that is going on."

"Thanks for not saying anything about the Grant kid," Sam stated.

"I figure until you know something definite, there is no need to stir up false hope." I admitted. "But it's more than a little unnerving knowing it could be him and he lives that close to me!"

"Do you want me to ask Chase to come stay with you?"

"That's a tempting thought but I'm OK. Besides, I've got Molly and I'm sure she will protect me," I stated lightheartedly.

"Right!" he chuckled.

We finished the afternoon sitting on the bench enjoying the warm sunshine and watching Molly run and play in the lot behind the apartments. Sam tossed her ball and she caught it in the air almost every time. "She's really getting good at that." He noted.

When it was time to go inside Sam asked for tuna sandwiches. While I made the tuna salad, he called the office to check for information on Jeffery Grant. "What did you find out?" I asked as we sat down to eat.

"They are still gathering information on him but he wasn't the one at the park yesterday. Hicks was here interviewing him while all that was going on."

"Oh," I responded with disappointment. "I was really hoping it was him so this could be over."

90

"I'm sorry. I know this is tough for you. I wish I could make it go away." Sam said, his voice resonated with compassion. "I know you don't want to hear this, but we could be dealing with two people; maybe Mr. X has teamed up with someone else. It bothers me that the second victim was stabbed while the other two were strangled. Everything else seems to be the same in all three slayings; it's just that one difference." He mused.

"Thanks for making me feel better," I said sarcastically. Sam just shook his head.

Chapter 27
Monday, March 13

Linda met me at the front door of the school with a big smile on her face. "I knew you were wrong about him. And, just for the record, I am not sorry I talked to him. You were miserable. He was miserable. Poor man had no clue; but I straightened him out!" she boasted.

"Well, 'just for the record', I'm not sorry you talked to him either. I still find it hard to believe that anyone would really be interested in me." I responded honestly.

"Don't cut yourself short. You have a lot to offer the right man. Besides, Reynolds definitely deserves a good woman. He's a great guy. You two are a perfect match," she countered sincerely.

"Let's don't let this conversation get too out of hand," I cautioned. "He likes me and I like him. Let's just leave it at that for the time being."

"OK," she threw her hands up in mock frustration. "Hey, what's all this I hear about a suspect living in your apartments?" And," she paused, "he showed up at the park? You had some weekend!"

I filled her in on all the details of Saturday's events. "Sam says there could be two killers." I concluded my story.

"That *is* a possibility. We've been kicking that around at the station." She admitted. The bell rang and ended any further conversation about the whole matter. Ronnie and Tim were the first ones in the door. They were holding a large brown paper sack between them.

"What do you guys have here?" I asked cautiously.

"Ronnie did it," informed Tim.

"Guess what is it," challenged Ronnie.

"Oh my! Do I get any hints?" I asked. Ronnie had brought surprises from home before. It could be anything from a piece of fruit to a frog or a rock he found.

"Nooo," they both answered in unison.

"Hey fellas," Linda chimed in. "Do I need to take it outside to open it?"

They both giggled. "NO!" Ronnie replied as he put his free hand up to his forehead. "It's for baby birds."

"Oh, I bet I know," I smiled. By now, all the kids had come in the room and were gathered around expectantly. "Does it have sticks?" I asked.

"Yes."

"Is it shaped like a bowl?"

"Yes!" They were getting excited.

"Is it brown?"

"YES! YES!" They were jumping up and down.

"Is it a bird nest?" I finally guessed.

"You got it! Carter got it," they hugged each other. Ronnie thrust the sack at me. "Open it!" he commanded.

Carefully I unfolded the top of the sack. In dramatic fashion, I pulled out the fully intact bird nest. There were lots of "oohs" and "ahhs" from the on-lookers. "Ronnie, this is beautiful!" I exclaimed. "You must have been very careful when you picked it up," I observed.

"Yep." He gloated thrusting out his chest.

"My home," said Randy.

"No, Randy. You cannot take it home. We are going to put it in the Nature area." I carefully placed the nest on the table by the window near my desk.

"How did you know what it was?" Linda questioned quietly.

"Mainly because in the class newsletter I sent home with the kids last Friday I told parents that this week we would be focusing on, among other things, the color brown and the letter 'N'. And he has brought things before that went along with our themes for the week."

Oh, right! I forgot about the newsletter."

Sam was there to pick me up after school. "You want to go get that ice cream we didn't get Saturday?"

I started laughing. "Sure. Let me guess, it's the best in the county."

"You're making fun of me now." He sounded hurt.

"I'm sorry, Sam. That's one of the things I love about you." I reached over and patted his arm.

"Really?" He brightened. "Just one?"

"Don't push your luck," I teased.

My hot fudge sundae, topped with a mound of whipped cream and a sprinkling of nuts, was a delicious treat. Sam indulged in a huge banana split. We ate in the car because the Dairy Bar did not have a dining room. "I have to tell you something," he said between mouthfuls.

"What's that?" I asked.

"I have to go back to the office after I drop you off. I have work I need to catch up on," he informed me apologetically.

"Oh, so you just brought me here to sweeten me up so I wouldn't be upset with you!" I accused, raising my eyebrows.

"Did it work?" he teased back. "I brought you here because I wanted to spend some time with you." He defended himself.

"OK. I guess you're off the hook." I responded, "*This* time."

Sam pulled in to the parking space in front of the apartments. "You don't need to walk me up. I'm OK." I told him.

"Alright, but I'll wait until you are inside." He responded.

I unlocked the apartment door and pushed it open as I looked around to wave goodbye. I turned back to enter and I stopped dead in my tracks. The dining table had been pulled out several feet away from the wall and in the middle of it sat a package wrapped in brown paper with green writing on it. I spun around to see Sam pulling out of the parking space. I waved hysterically and fell to my knees unable to speak. Sam threw the car in Park, jumped out and bounded up the stairs two at a time. He entered the apartment and after a few minutes came back to me on the landing. He squatted down beside me. "There's nobody in there now. The box had a green leash and a note. 'Sorry you didn't like the rope'." He relayed. "Come on," he encouraged me. "Let's go in and sit on the couch."

"NO! I...c-can't. He... was...h-here..." My voice rasped between sobs. "He... was..." I grabbed Sam's arms, "Where's Molly?" I demanded frantically.

"She's OK. She is still in the kitchen. Come on in and sit down. I'll get her for you," he said calmingly. He pulled me up to a standing position.

"I can't!" I stood rooted to the spot. "H-He..." Suddenly everything went black.

I was aware of the faint sound of voices. I opened my eyes. I was lying on my bed with the blanket pulled up to my waist. Linda was sitting on the edge of the bed petting Molly. "Welcome back." She smiled.

"What happened?" I questioned.

"Reynolds said you passed out on him."

"Where is he?"

"In the living room talking to Hicks and Reed." She got up and walked out of the room. Fifteen seconds later, Sam came in and sat on the edge of the bed.

94

"How are you feeling?" He asked, tenderly touching my cheek with the back of his hand.

"Kind of foggy. How long have I been asleep?"

"A little over an hour. You fainted outside and I brought you in here. The table was moved and there was a package on it. Do you remember?" he asked gently.

"Ummm, yes," I answered slowly.

"The table was moved because the maintenance man came in to check the thermostat on the wall heater. When the transformer blew out the other night it messed up some of them in other apartments so he was checking all the units to make sure they were functioning correctly. The package was in front of your door when he came up so he just brought it in and left it on the table. So, Mr. X was not actually *in* your apartment." He explained. "I am going to have to go but Chase is going to stay with you tonight." He added apologetically.

"Oh Sam, she doesn't..."

"No arguing." He put his finger to my lips. "You are going to stay in bed and get some rest. She will be here if you need anything. That's an order." He smiled.

"OK," I agreed reluctantly.

He leaned over and kissed me on the forehead. "I'll see you in the morning."

Chapter 28
Tuesday, March 14

Sam arrived at five thirty so Linda could go home and get ready for school. He stood at my bedroom door and called, "Hey sleepyhead! Are you going to stay in bed all day?"

"What time is it?" I blinked at the clock but couldn't quite focus enough to read it.

"Five thirty-eight," was his chipper reply.

"Come back at six. That's when the alarm goes off." I moaned.

"You are going to make me eat donuts and drink coffee all by myself?" he countered.

"OK. OK. I'll be there in a minute." I grumbled. Sam laughed and closed the door. I got up and slipped on my robe and house shoes. Sam had a cup of coffee sitting on the table waiting for me. Beside it was a napkin with two glazed donuts laying on it.

He smiled broadly. "Good morning!"

"You are way too happy this morning." I accused. "What are you doing here so early?"

"Chase needed some time to get ready for the day so I came to relieve her. What did you girls do last night?"

"Not much. We talked. Linda ordered us a pizza. We ate it in the bedroom because she said you told her not to let me get up. What's with that?"

"You've been through a lot lately, in case you hadn't noticed. Your system has had more than its share of shocks and upsets. I know you have not been sleeping. I figured if you responded yesterday by passing out; your body is saying it needs some rest." He diagnosed. "Thus, my instructions," he added with a wave of his hand.

"Thanks, Doctor Reynolds," I responded sleepily.

He reached across the table and took my hand. "I really wish you would stay home today."

"I can't, Sam. Besides, it's really better for me to stay busy – it helps keep my mind off things."

"OK," he relented. "I'll tell you what... I will take Molly downstairs while you get dressed. Is half an hour enough time?"

"That will be fine." I concurred. "Take my key so you can let yourself back in." I jumped in the shower as soon as I heard the door shut. I had just finished drying my hair and started brushing my teeth when I heard the key turning in the lock.

"Are you decent?" he called from the front door.

"Yes, come on in," I answered from the bathroom with my mouth full of toothpaste. I rinsed my mouth, dried my hands and walked into the living room. "You realize I am ready a full hour before I normally leave for school. I could have slept another forty-five minutes or so!"

"Come sit with me on the couch," he invited.

"Will you sing to me?" I asked.

"What would you like to hear?" he smiled.

"It Is Well With My Soul," was my quick reply.

He opened his arms and I snuggled in beside him. With my head on his shoulder and his arms around me, he started to sing softly. Peace flooded my soul.

All too soon, it was time to go. Grudgingly I got my coat and purse. Sam set up the gate for Molly. "You sure you don't want to stay home?" he asked. I shook my head and sighed.

The throbbing started in my temples shortly after I got to school. The painful ache increased in intensity throughout the morning until my whole head was pounding. By lunchtime, I decided I needed to go home. Linda insisted on calling Sam to pick me up rather than me walking the short distance home.

"You don't need to be walking around when you can't even focus on what you're doing." She asserted.

Sam offered to stay with me for a while but I declined. "I'm just going to bed and sleep. Besides, you have too much to do at the station." I reminded him.

"OK," he agreed. "You go on to bed. I'll take Molly out for you and then come back later and check on you."

"That sounds like a wonderful plan." I handed him my key and headed for the bedroom. Sleep came faster than I had expected. I did not even hear Sam when he brought Molly back.

I woke up a little after three; my head sore but at least not hurting. I went to the kitchen to get a glass of milk and some chocolate chip cookies.

"Hey girl," I greeted Molly as I took down the gate. "Would you like a treat while I eat a snack?" I offered her a dog biscuit, which she eagerly accepted. I sat down at the table and looked at the calendar while I munched. As I studied the dates and events, I began to notice a pattern. "I never considered that before," I said to the cookie I had just dunked in the milk. I started writing down dates and figuring the timeline.

I heard the key in the lock. Sam eased the door open. "Oh, you're up," he noted with surprise. "How are you feeling?"

"Better, my head isn't hurting. I am glad you are here. Come look at this," I encouraged.

He walked over to the table. "Have any more milk and cookies?" He asked hopefully.

"Sure. Help yourself."

"Sam," I said as he went in the kitchen. "I think I know who is next and when it is supposed to happen."

"What do you mean?" he came back with a glass of milk and a stack of cookies.

"Look," I pointed at the calendar. "The murders all happened on the second day after the new moon. And the victim's birthdays were the one closest to that second day."

"Hmmm, very interesting." Sam studied the calendar. "How did you come up with that?"

"See the little symbols in the lower left corner of the date squares?" I indicated the places for him to look. "They show the phases of the moon. I am next. He will show up Friday." I declared numbly.

"NO," Sam denied.

"Sam, my birthday is *tomorrow*; it's the new moon. Friday is two days later." I shuddered.

"We'll be ready for him, this time. He is *not* going to hurt you or anybody else, ever again." He insisted fervently.

"What are you going to do?" I lifted my hands in hopelessness.

"I'll have a man in your apartment around the clock starting tomorrow morning or maybe Thursday morning since you don't expect him until Friday. Chase can come and stay with you overnight. That way if Mr. X is watching he will see the two of you leave every morning and he won't suspect that there is someone still inside."

I could see Sam working out all the details in his mind as he sat there rubbing his chin. "Then Friday when he tries to come in, we'll get him."

"Would you forgive me if I said that doesn't really make me feel any better?" I asked. "I don't know what's worse...not knowing when or what is going to happen; or knowing when it's supposed to happen and having to wait." I added. "What if he doesn't try to come in here? What if he comes to the school? What if he…"

"Janet," Sam reached for my hand. "It doesn't matter where he is; I am going to be right there with you. *Nothing* is going to happen to you." His eyes riveted on mine; as mine started to fill up with tears. Sam stood up. "Come on. Let's go."

"Where are we going?"

"Driving around. I want to get you out of here for a while." He got Molly's leash; hooked her up and opened the door. The country roads were lined with thick woods on both sides. I could see the Redbud and Dogwood trees spreading their delicate colors among the tall Pines and bare branches of other trees that were starting to bud out. Sam turned off the main road on to a gravel road that had a slight incline. We drove for a mile or so and came to a clearing on the top of a hill. Sam unhooked Molly's leash and set her down on the ground. She spotted a squirrel a short distance away and took out after it. We laughed as she jumped and barked at the base of the tree where the squirrel took its refuge. "This is beautiful," I noted as I looked around at the sunlight dancing through the branches.

"Take a look over here." Sam led me to the edge of the hill. Below was an open field with a stream running through the middle of it. The sunlight reflected like sparkling diamonds on the swiftly moving water. We made our way down the side of the hill; the sound of the babbling stream becoming louder as we approached.

"I love that sound!" I exclaimed. "I could listen to that forever."

"Have a seat," Sam indicated a large rock near the stream. He sat on the grass beside me. Molly came tumbling down the hill; thrilled at all the space she had to run.

"I should have brought her ball," I said regretfully.

Sam reached in his pocket, pulled out her ball and flung it hard for her to chase. I looked at him with astonishment. "What?" He exclaimed with a smile. "I was a Boy Scout!"

"You never cease to amaze me," I admitted, shaking my head.

"Good. I like to keep you guessing." He chuckled.

Chapter 29
Wednesday, March 15

Sam arrived at six thirty-five with a dozen peach colored roses and a sack from the Donut Hole. He stepped in the door and started singing. "Sam, these are beautiful!" I fussed over the roses when he finished his birthday song. "And they smell heavenly! Thank you so much," I gave him a peck on the cheek.

He handed me the donut sack. "I got you something special," he smiled proudly. "It's an apple fritter. It will taste really great with a glass of cold milk." He hinted.

"Did you get one for yourself, too?" I inquired as I looked at the two pastries in the sack.

"Well, yeah! We both can get special treats on your birthday." He replied with a grin.

"You are too funny! I'll get the milk and glasses. Do you want coffee, too?"

"No, I think the milk will be all I want." He decided. We sat down and started eating the apple fritters.

The crisp glazed outside and tender inside filled with small bits of apple were melt-in-your-mouth delicious. "These are good! Why haven't you brought them before?"

"Saving them for a special occasion." He winked.

"Like my last birthday?" I asked pessimistically.

"Don't spoil today thinking like that." He said sadly.

"I'm sorry, Sam but it sort of keeps popping up in my mind. I can't help it." I responded truthfully.

"I understand. Nevertheless, you just remember, today is special because it is the first birthday, of many more to come, that I am spending with you. And I intend to make it your best one yet!" He promised. "Oh, and I made reservations for tonight at Shirley's in Halmont. Are you ready for a really good steak?" He raised his eyebrows. "What cut do you prefer?"

"Rib eye would be my steak of choice, but I am open for any suggestions you might have."

"Oh, excellent choice! They have absolutely the best marinated rib-eye I have ever put in my mouth. You're going to love it!" he exclaimed enthusiastically.

The Birthday Killer

"OK," I laughed. "Are you going to take Molly out for me so I can get my stuff together?" I inquired.

"No, you need to go with me. I'm supposed to stall your arrival." He said mysteriously.

"What?"

"You aren't supposed to get to your room until after the bell rings." He indicated.

"Why?"

"Stop asking questions and just follow directions." He commanded.

"Yes, sir!" I saluted.

Sam deposited me in the front office when we got to school. "Keep her here for ten minutes." He told Mrs. Post. I just shrugged my shoulders and shook my head. He started out the door and then turned back. "Oh, make a little noise in the hall before you come in," he informed me.

I stopped outside my classroom door and coughed. I heard Linda urging everyone to be quiet. "Shhh. I think she is coming. Get ready... Randy you are supposed to be hiding. Mr. Sam, could you help Donna hold the sign?" I waited a few more seconds to make sure they were ready. The lights were off when I opened the door.

"I wonder where everyone is." I said loudly as I flipped on the light switch. All the kids with Sam and Linda leading, jumped out from where they were hiding and yelled, "Surprise!"

"Oh, my! What is going on here?" I feigned extreme surprise. The kids were all laughing and swarmed me while shouting various birthday greetings.

"I made cake!" exclaimed Ronnie pulling me over to the table. He pointed proudly to an oblong cake decorated with sky blue icing and one big red candle in the middle.

"Hap day!" squealed Toni.

"My baby Carter," Randy hugged me.

"Me present," smiled Tina broadly while waving a white tissue paper covered box with multicolored flowers drawn on it.

Linda and Sam just stood back and laughed at the spectacle. Donna had apparently left the sign holding entirely up to Sam. She was jumping up and down, clapping her hands while he held a white butcher paper sign with handprints made by each student in various colors of tempera paint with their name scrawled underneath in magic marker.

Sam excused himself shortly after eight thirty. Linda had planned birthday games to play all morning. At lunchtime, she had pizza delivered for the whole class and we ate the cake for dessert. The kids were a little rowdy with all the unusual activities but it turned out to be a very enjoyable day that went by rather quickly. Sam was waiting when I walked out the front door.

I changed clothes while Sam took Molly outside. After rejecting three other outfits, I finally settled on a navy blue linen, A-line skirt with a matching jacket. I paired it with a yellow, red, and blue floral, long sleeve, silk blouse. Sam gave a low whistle when he and Molly came back inside. "Wow! You look great," he exclaimed.

"Thanks," I smiled back. Sam secured Molly in the kitchen and we headed out.

The forty-five minute drive was quiet and tranquil. Sam held my hand and hummed most of the way to Halmont. I rested my head on his shoulder, relaxing in the comfort of his presence, trying not to think about what was in store for me on Friday. Just before we arrived at the restaurant Sam broke the spell.

"What did Tina give you?"

"It was a box of four fancy handkerchiefs. The kind with lace around the edges and a flower embroidered in one of the corners. Made me feel like a real teacher," I noted with a smile.

"How so?" He quizzed.

"When I was growing up that was what we gave our teachers for Christmas; pretty handkerchiefs. I did not realize they still made them but I like it. It was sort of an affirmation that I am where I am supposed to be."

Sam had reserved, not surprisingly, a corner table. The table, draped with an ivory colored linen tablecloth, hosted a Waterford crystal vase on one corner, filled with a beautiful arrangement of burgundy colored roses that harmonized with the like colored linen napkins that were folded in the center of white china plates trimmed with a thin band of gold around the edges. A single tapered burgundy candle set in a matching Waterford crystal candlestick graced the center of our table. I noticed as we were led to our seats that each table in the dimly lit dining room was surrounded by strategically placed graceful Weeping Fig plants, Corn Plants, Peace Lilies, and other lightly flowering plants to provide an intimate privacy. Softly playing violin music completed the romantic atmosphere.

"I have never been surrounded by such elegance," I confessed in awe.

"An elegant place for an elegant lady." His blue eyes twinkled as he smiled. Sam placed our order for marinated rib eye, baked potatoes and salad. When I requested lemonade, the waiter suggested their special blend of Strawberry Lemonade. He returned almost instantly with our drinks and salad. The lemonade was a delicate mix of crushed strawberries and hand-squeezed lemons. It was not overly sweet and offered a delightful flavor for a new beverage experience. The thick and creamy Bleu Cheese dressing enhanced the flavor of the fresh garden salad. The bold rich taste had obviously not come from a bottle.

The marinated rib eye was definitely not a disappointment. I had never before tasted such a tender and flavorful piece of meat. Sam informed me that the Shirley's raised their own grass-fed cattle for the restaurant; guaranteeing its freshness. The portions were huge and I had half of the steak and baked potato left to take home for another meal. Sam ordered a piece of Turtle Cheesecake to take with us. "We can share it when we get home," he suggested.

The drive back to Lakin was without incident but enjoyable nonetheless. Sam sang "Happy Birthday" repeatedly. I made him stop after the fourth time. "I just want to make sure today is a special day for you," he explained mischievously.

"OK. I got it. Thank you. You have definitely made this a day to remember. But if you really want to sing I can think of a few other songs I would rather hear."

"Fine." He pretended to be insulted. "How about..." He began to sing "I'll Be There" by the Jackson 5.

"Oh, that's better," I snuggled in beside him. When he had finished the song I said, "I love it when you sing to me. *That* is what really makes me feel special."

"Happy Bir..." he started singing.

"NO! I do not want to hear that one again." I thumped him on the arm and he started laughing. "I'm not going to share the cheesecake with you, if you're not careful." I threatened.

"OK, I'll be good." He promised; still laughing.

When we got back to my apartment, we both took Molly outside. We sat on the bench watching while she ran around the lot. "Sam," I asked quietly, "will you take care of Molly if I'm not here?"

He turned to face me. "I thought we weren't going to think like that."

"I can't help it, Sam. Today has been the most wonderful day of my life and I am thankful that God has allowed you to be a major part of it. I'm not trying to spoil anything but I can't pretend that the last few weeks haven't happened." My eyes filled with tears. "Mr. X is planning to end everything for me in two days. That is the truth of the situation that we are facing at the moment. I trust you completely but what if he does something to you?" I shivered in the chilly night air. Sam put his arms around me and pulled me close. "I wish this moment could last forever," I whispered.

Sam stared at the moonless sky; I knew he was thinking about how to respond. His arms tightened around me and he made a soft groan. "Janet, I can't stand the thought of losing you... for any reason. Nevertheless, even knowing how *I* feel about all of this doesn't begin to give me any real understanding about how hard this is for you. I want to make it go away. I want to stop all of this torment for you. In that respect, I feel utterly helpless. But I know in my heart that, by the grace of God, we will come out on the other side of this... together." He pulled away and held me by my shoulders. "Janet," He said huskily, his voice full of emotion, "I love you! I will do anything and everything possible to keep you safe."

"Oh, Sam. God has blessed me way more than I deserve by giving me someone as wonderful as you." I whispered as the tears slid down my cheeks. "You are my knight in shining armor. Thank you for a delightful day and most especially for a perfect time tonight."

He wiped my tears away with his thumbs as he gently held my face with his hands. "You are more than welcome," was his response as he leaned over and kissed me tenderly.

Chapter 30
Thursday, March 16

I lay awake long before the alarm went off, smiling to myself while thinking of the evening before with Sam. He was a sensitive, thoughtful man who obviously cared a great deal for me; a perfect gentleman who made me feel like I was the only woman in the world. I thought about all we had been through together and I finally admitted to myself what I already knew; that I loved him, too. I was not sure why I was so hesitant to tell him how I felt. Maybe it was because I still found it difficult to believe that anyone as magnificent as Sam would love me and I was afraid I would wake up and find it was just a lovely dream.

Molly stood up beside the bed and whimpered. "Come on up, girl." I patted the space beside me. She jumped up on the bed and curled up next to me. "Are you wanting to go outside already?" I asked her. Her ears perked up and she answered with an excited bark. "OK, sweetie. Let me get dressed and I'll take you out." I slipped on my clothes for the day and we made the short walk to the back lot. She wasted no time taking care of business. "I guess you really did have to go!" I observed as I threw the ball for her to chase. After several more throws, we headed back inside.

Sam was climbing the stairs as we rounded the corner. "You're out early! Why didn't you wait for me?" He called down to us.

"Sometimes a girl just can't wait." I informed him with a smile. Molly danced all around Sam when we caught up to him.

I made cinnamon toast for breakfast after we got back inside. "Have you got any peanut butter to put on these?" Sam asked as he took a bite out of his first piece.

"Sure," I responded reaching into the cabinet to grab the jar. "I never had peanut butter on cinnamon toast before,"

"Try it. I bet you will like it," he encouraged.

I put a little dab on one corner of my toast. "Mmm, that *is* good," I said in surprise and started spreading more peanut butter on the rest of the piece. "You are just full of new dining insights! I can't wait to see what you do with bologna and cheese," I teased.

"You just wait, missy. I have a few more tricks up my sleeve." He chuckled mysteriously.

Linda was just getting out of her car when Sam dropped me off at school. "I want to know *every* detail of your evening." She informed me as we walked in the front door.

"And just who is *this* report going to?" I inquired with a smile.

"We have to keep up with him somehow. He's not talking and the guys are depending on me," she defended enthusiastically with a quick laugh.

"What makes you think if he's not talking that I will?" I shot back at her. We bantered back and forth good-naturedly down the hall.

"You're not going to tell me anything, are you?" She said with resignation.

"I will tell you this…we had a great time. The steak was absolutely the best I have ever had. I don't know what they do to it but it was divine!"

"He didn't propose or anything?" She quizzed with exasperated disappointment.

"What?" I choked on a laugh. "Why in the world would you think he would propose to me? We have not even known each other that long. Your romantic fantasy is definitely working overtime! You probably already have the wedding planned," I accused lightheartedly. I was not about to share Sam's declaration of love for me. That was for me to cherish and hold close to my heart for the time being.

The bell rang and our day began. A few minutes before nine o'clock I sat down at my desk to make out the lunch report. I opened the top drawer to get a pen. I jumped back, banging my chair against the wall and gasped, "LINDA!" Suddenly, I could not breathe. The room got instantly quiet; the kids all turned to look at me.

"What's wrong?" Linda rushed over. I was struggling to get a breath. Linda looked in my drawer and saw the yellow paper with a message written in all capital letters. She put one hand on my shoulder and slowly closed the drawer with the other. "It's OK guys," she addressed the class. "It's just a spider in her drawer that jumped out and scared her. Everything is fine." Reassured, the kids went back to their activities. Linda turned to me and spoke quietly. "Janet, you're OK. I will get rid of that in a minute. Take a deep breath…slowly…that's right…just relax." She coached.

"I think I am going to be sick. I've got to get out of here," I cautioned with alarm.

"Go ahead. I've got this."

I rushed out the door at the end of the hall near my room and sat on the steps of the covered porch. I was numb to the cold air that swirled around the corner of the building. Tears started flowing as I locked my arms around my knees and started rocking back and forth. Gradually my nausea subsided. I hoped there would not be any classes coming out to the playground anytime soon to disturb my reverie. I do not know how long I had been sitting there when the door opened. Sam came and sat down beside me. He gathered me into his arms and held me tight. He did not say a word; just sat there with me. Slowly, I began to regain my senses; my breathing became less labored and my heartbeat returned to a normal rhythm.

"He was in my room, Sam. How did he get in my room?"

"I have men working on that right now. However, my concern is that you are OK. Do I need to take you home?" He spoke quietly; his voice full of compassion.

"I don't know where I want to be right now," I admitted; my mind still reeling.

"Take all the time you need to decide. I am here as long as you need me."

We sat in silence for a while. "Sam?"

"Yes."

"What did the note say?"

"It said, 'Hope you enjoyed your last birthdate. Get ready. I will be coming to see you soon.'" I shuddered. Sam's muscles tightened. "He just better hope someone else gets to him first. I can't guarantee that I won't forget my position and how I should be handling the situation." His voice was tense with anger.

There was a tap on the door. It opened slightly, "Chief, can I talk to you for a minute?"

"Yeah, Hicks. I'll be there in just a minute." Sam answered.

"Did he just call you 'Chief'?" I pulled away to look at him.

"Yes, we'll talk about that later. Are you ready to go back inside or do you want to stay out here?"

"I guess I'll go back to the room. I need to check on the kids…and Linda."

A uniformed officer, I deduced to be Hicks, was standing just inside the door as we walked back inside. He nodded and stepped outside.

I walked to my door, took a deep breath and looked back at Sam who was holding the outside door open watching me. He smiled and nodded reassuringly, "I'm here if you need me."

The kids were all seated on the big rug in the center of the room listening to Linda reading them a story. "We stayed longer in centers this morning," she stopped to explain. "I took some extra time to take care of things so we are a little off schedule."

"Miss Linda kill that spider," announced Tim.

"Yeah," said Ronnie in amazement. "She smash him," he declared as he slapped his hands together in demonstration.

"Thank you, Miss Linda for taking care of that for me," I said sincerely.

"Any time," She smiled. Linda returned to reading the story. I sat at the kidney-shaped table and listened. A few minutes later Sam stepped in and the kids yelled greetings, interrupting Linda's story for a second time.

"Sorry guys," he waved and smiled. "I didn't mean to disturb you. Carry on," he directed. He turned to me. "Do you have time to talk?"

"The kids go to lunch in about ten minutes," I said checking my watch. "Can you wait? Linda can take them and I can stay here."

"Sure, that's not a problem." He sat down at the table with me. Linda finished the story and the kids all cheered. After a short discussion about the book, they lined up and headed to the cafeteria. When the door closed behind them, Sam took out a small notebook from his inside coat pocket and turned to face me.

"Hicks had two bits of information for me. First, Jeffery Grant, the man with the green towel, has a solid alibi for every incident. He is no longer a suspect. Second, he got a timeline from Mr. Walker for this morning. Walker got here at five thirty and made rounds to make sure everything was secure. At six o'clock, he opened the outside kitchen door and let the cafeteria workers in. At six fifteen, he unlocked all the classroom doors. At seven, he unlocked the front doors and returned to the kitchen to get some coffee. At seven fifteen, he was in the gym to wait for early arriving students. Walker says he did not see anyone in the building during that time. Mr. X apparently had about a fifteen-minute window of opportunity from seven o'clock to seven fifteen to enter the building, go to your room, leave the note and make his escape. He probably exited out the door at the end of the hall by your room."

I just stared at Sam for a few minutes; my mind racing. "He had to be watching… for more than just today. I am guessing Mr. Walker has pretty much the same schedule every day. For Mr. X to be able to know when was the right time to get in and do what he wanted without getting caught; he had to be watching." I shuddered. "So what now?" I looked at him helplessly.

"I have had men watching your apartment since we left this morning. I need to get your key so I can put Jackson inside. Chase will come over

108

when I leave this evening and stay overnight. Jackson will stay in your apartment in case anyone tries to get in during the day."

I stood up and started toward my desk to get my key. I froze. I could not make my feet move any closer to my desk. Sam came and stood behind me, wrapping his arms around me. "Chase checked out all the drawers. There are no more surprises in there."

"Would you get my purse for me, please? It's in the bottom drawer."

Sam retrieved my purse and I handed him my key. We walked up the hall together. He left with the promise to pick me up at the end of the day. I went to the cafeteria.

True to his word, Sam was waiting for me in front of the building when it was time to go home. We stopped by the grocery store to get bread, lunchmeat, and chips so Jackson would have something to eat while he was staying in my apartment. When we arrived, Sam unlocked the door, opened it a bit and said, "Stand down, Jackson."

"Clear," came a voice from behind the door.

We entered to be greeted by a tall, thin blond-headed man in his late twenties. "Janet, this is Officer Steve Jackson. Jackson, Janet Carter." Sam made the introductions. "Hope you like ham sandwiches; that's what you'll be having for the next few days."

"Works for me Chief," Jackson replied as he shook my hand. "Nice to meet you Miss Carter."

"What is this 'chief' business?" I looked at Sam.

"Chief Marshall, the *current* chief," Sam looked pointedly at Jackson, "has been in poor health the last six months or so. He has decided to retire at the end of the month. Apparently, at the City Council meeting last Tuesday night, they voted me in as his replacement. The mayor called me in this morning to let me know. The guys are jumping the gun just a bit." He explained.

"You've been doing his job for the last four months anyway." Jackson retorted. "You may as well be using his title, too."

"I don't officially become 'Chief' until the first day of April but I am assuming his duties immediately." Sam clarified.

"Congratulations," I offered. "Are you coming with me to take Molly out or do you need to stay here and talk to Officer Jackson?" I asked.

"I'm coming with you."

Molly seemed a little subdued as she sniffed around the lot. She kept looking back at Sam and me. "I think she is a little confused by all the extra activity in the apartment," I surmised. "She is definitely not behaving in her usual exuberant way."

"Amen to that. She was excited when I first brought Jackson in earlier but she quieted down pretty fast when it was apparent he was going to be staying. I think she was a little intimidated by his sleeping bag." Sam laughed. "She kept sniffing it and jumping away like she thought it was going to grab her or something."

I leaned against Sam and put my head on his shoulder. I let out a big sigh, "I am so tired. I know it is more emotional than physical but it affects me the same way."

"I thought maybe we would go get a burger or something but if you want to stay in I can order a pizza." Sam offered.

"I really would like for you to just hold me but I don't think I would be comfortable with Officer Jackson around." I told him truthfully.

"OK, then we'll go out for a while. Any place you want to go?"

"I love that meadow with the stream running through it but it's a little late to go there, isn't it?" I suggested.

"Yes, it really is. I was kind of planning to go there one day next week for a picnic while you're off for Spring Break." He replied. "How about the park? I'll make sure no one follows us there."

"OK," I conceded. "That'll be fine."

Sam called Molly and we returned to the apartment. After briefing Officer Jackson, we headed to the park. "Chicken or burgers?" Sam asked.

"I don't want anything. I'm really not hungry."

"Did you eat anything for lunch today?"

"No." I shook my head.

"Cinnamon toast is not enough for all day. You *will* eat something. Now, what do you want?" He insisted firmly.

"Sam, please don't force me to make a decision. I am just not up to it. Whatever you get will be fine with me." I pleaded quietly.

"OK," his voice softened. "I'm going for chicken."

We pulled into the parking lot at the park as the only remaining car was leaving. The last rays of the sun were quickly fading. "Do you want to eat at a table?" he asked.

"Not really. I would rather just stay in the car. I'm sorry; I'm not very good company tonight." I apologized.

"You are just fine." His fingers caressed my cheek. "We will have a cozy little meal right here," he smiled.

After a few bites of chicken and a roll, I sipped on my lemonade while Sam finished eating. He got out to throw away our trash and when he returned he held his arms open, "I am at your disposal." I snuggled close to him. His arms wrapped tenderly around me, giving me a welcomed sense of protection and security. His rich voice quietly filled the car.

"Why should I be discouraged, why should the shadows fall?
Why should my heart be lonely, and long for heaven and home?
When Jesus is my portion, my constant Friend is He,
His eye is on the sparrow and I know He watches me.
His eye is on the sparrow and I know He watches me.

> I sing because I'm happy;
> I sing because I'm free;
> His eye is on the sparrow
> And I know He watches me.

'Let not your heart be troubled'; these tender words I hear;
And resting on his goodness I lose my doubts and fears;
For by the path He leadeth but one step I may see;
His eye is on the sparrow and I know He watches me.
His eye is on the sparrow and I know He watches me.

> I sing because I'm happy;
> I sing because I'm free;
> His eye is on the sparrow
> And I know He watches me.

Whenever I am tempted; whenever clouds arise;
When songs give place to sighing; when hope within me dies;
I draw the closer to Him; from care He sets me free;
His eye is on the sparrow and I know He watches me.
His eye is on the sparrow and I know He watches me.

> I sing because I'm happy;
> I sing because I'm free;
> His eye is on the sparrow
> And I know He watches me."[5]

---

[5] "His Eye Is On The Sparrow", Civilla D. Martin, Public Domain

Chapter 31
Friday, March 17

Sam radioed dispatch on our way back to the apartment to have them contact Linda to meet us there. She pulled in just as we were getting out of the car. As we climbed the stairs, I addressed them both. "Would you guys mind terribly if I just went straight to bed? I am really tired!"

"Of course, that's OK!" Linda exclaimed. "I'll take Molly out while you say good night to Reynolds."

"Thanks Chase. You're a real trouper," laughed Sam. When he unlocked the door, again he said, "Stand down, Jackson."

"Clear," Jackson replied.

Molly was ready to go outside when Linda got her leash. "See you in a few," she called as she went out the door. Jackson went to the kitchen to get a snack and I headed for the bedroom. Sam followed me to the bedroom door.

"Goodnight, my sweet. I hope you feel better in the morning. Try to get some rest." He kissed my forehead. I leaned against him; I did not really want him to leave.

"Good night, Sam. Thank you for being here. I'll see you in the morning." I fell asleep fairly quickly. The next thing I was aware of was the alarm going off at six o'clock. I put on my robe and slippers and checked to see if anyone else was up. Jackson was curled up in his sleeping bag near the front door and Sam was sitting on the couch with Molly in his lap.

"Good morning, beautiful. How are you feeling?" he asked with a smile.

"Definitely better, thanks. What time did you get here?"

"About ten after five. Chase made coffee before she left, if you want some."

I nodded and headed for the kitchen. I got a cup of coffee and went back to sit beside Sam on the couch. "You didn't bring donuts?" I asked.

"I think Chase put some in the oven for you so Jackson wouldn't eat them all." He informed me. I went back to the kitchen, retrieved the donuts and returned to the couch. "I'm going to make a cop out of you yet!" he laughed. "Are you going to school today?"

"Yes, I have to see my kids one more time... just in case." I said seriously.

Sam winced. "You'll see them again after Spring Break, I promise."

"It's not that I don't believe you Sam, but you can't make that kind of promise. My heart says you are right but my head says we are not in control of what happens today. Maybe it is just *me* that is not in control. I am scared and I can't help it. I am trying to come to terms with the fact that today might be my last day alive."

Sam put his arms around me and quietly prayed. "Heavenly Father, please help Janet to have Your peace. Help her to know that YOU are in control. Protect her Lord and keep her safe." I laid my head on his shoulder and wished this moment in his arms could last forever.

"Thank you, Sam." His arms pressed a little tighter. "Are you going to stay with me at school?"

"No, I can't. I have a meeting this morning with the Mayor and the President of the City Council. But as soon as I am finished with that, I will be there."

"OK," I said disappointedly. "I guess I better start getting ready."

"I'll take Molly out and give you some time. Don't worry about Jackson; he'll sleep until I wake him up before we leave."

"Did you get any donuts or did Jackson find them first?" Linda asked as I came in the front door.

"Yes, thank you for hiding some for me. He was sleeping when I got up. Sam said he laid back down right after he ate the last donut in the box, shortly after you left."

"That man can eat!" she exclaimed. "You may not have anything left in the cabinet *or* refrigerator when you get home!" she laughed.

The morning seemed to whiz by. I had Linda make out the lunch report. I could not bring myself to go near my desk. The kids were perfect in centers; no fussing or disagreements. We were just finishing the story for the day when Sam arrived bringing hamburgers for Linda, himself, and me.

"Why don't you two stay in here and eat. I'll take the kids to lunch." Linda offered.

"No, Linda. You took them yesterday. We can all go," I protested.

"But I really enjoy it," she argued. "Besides, I won't be here that much longer and then you'll have them all the time."

"OK," I relented. "But, you know you can always come back for a visit and eat lunch with us whenever you get a chance."

Sam and I sat down at the kidney shaped table. He held my hand while he said grace. "It's good to hear you speaking positively about the future," he smiled.

"I'm trying to be optimistic." I confessed. "What did the Mayor have to say?"

"Nothing I wasn't expecting. He just discussed my role in the department and wanted to know if I have any suggestions for improvement. I told him I'd get back with him after I gave it a little more thought."

"I was thinking about you staying here this afternoon." I mused. "I'm OK. You can go back to work." I suggested.

"Janet, it's OK. I can stay."

"I know you *can* stay, Sam. And I know you *would* stay if I asked you. However, we both know you have a lot of catching up to do. I take up too much of your time already."

"Hey, it's not every man that is lucky enough to have a job assignment that allows him to spend extra time with the woman he loves. I am not complaining. In fact, I am rather enjoying it right now." He said tenderly as he reached over and touched my cheek.

I held his hand against my cheek. "Oh, Sam, I...I...," the door opened and the kids came back from lunch. Randy came over and put his hand on my shoulder.

"MY Carter!" he said boldly. He put his other hand on his hip and glared at Sam.

Sam stifled at laugh. "You know Randy, you're right. I will make a deal with you. You can have her during the day at school and then it is my turn when school is over. What do you say? Is it a deal?" Sam held out his hand.

Randy was quiet for a minute, obviously considering Sam's proposition. Finally, he reached out and shook hands. "Okie," he agreed. The matter was settled.

"I always dreamed of two men fighting over me but somehow this is not exactly what I imagined." I shook my head in disbelief. Linda and Sam both broke out in laughter.

The afternoon was uneventful. We stayed on schedule for the remainder of the day. All too soon, it was time to go home. Sam greeted me with a smile at the front door of the school. "Your carriage awaits."

"Home, James." I responded.

"Sorry, James is on vacation. You're stuck with me." He laughed. "Where do you want to go?"

"Can we just go sit at the park for a little while?" I inquired.

"Of course we can!" He replied enthusiastically turning left out of the parking lot and heading toward Lakin Park. "Do you want to stop on the way and get something for supper?"

"No, it's too early for that. I just want to spend a little time alone with you." I confessed.

There was no one else at the park when we arrived. We walked to the center of the rose garden and sat on a bench by the goldfish pond. It was a beautiful afternoon with high fluffy clouds floating lazily in the sky. The warm sunshine felt good on my back as we made plans for the evening. "So you want to get fajitas to take back to your place and play games with Chase and Jackson?" Sam reviewed what we had discussed.

"Right. It is going to be a long evening and we may as well do something fun to help pass the time. I just wish you could stay all night. You know he won't show up if you are there. He'll wait until you leave before he tries anything." I said nervously.

"Tonight is all about you. Whatever you want, we will do." Sam said comfortingly.

When we got in the car, Sam radioed dispatch to call in two large orders for fajitas and all the trimmings so they would be ready when we got there to pick them up. He also told them to call Linda to come on over to my apartment. The Green Sombrero was as busy as it had been the first night we went there even though it was only five thirty. Sam locked me in the car while he went in to get our order. "I'll be right back," he promised. He returned promptly with two large bags.

"That's enough to feed a small army," I exclaimed.

"Or at least Jackson," he teased.

Linda was waiting when we arrived at the apartment. "I'm ready for some of that!" She said enthusiastically, looking at the sacks of food. "And a game night sounds like fun, too." She took my key and opened the door. "Stand down, Jackson."

"Clear," he replied.

We decided to set the food out buffet style in the kitchen. "There is still a lot of food in here," I observed when I took my dishes back to the kitchen. Sam had gotten seconds and Jackson had been back three times.

"I'll take care of that tomorrow," Jackson spoke up. "Uh, that is if no one else wants any of it." We all laughed.

W. Kay Lynn

We had just started playing a game of Scrabble when the telephone phone rang. Sam crossed the living room to answer it. "Hello. Yes, she is right here. I'll get her for you, Jerry." He turned to me, "Your brother wants to talk to you."

After a brief exchange of belated birthday wishes and small talk, I hung up the receiver. "He never could get my birthday right." I laughed as I started back to the table. The phone rang again. I turned and reached to pick it up. "Hello," I said brightly.

"I'm coming to see you," the muffled voice said. I whirled around with a gasp and thrust the phone toward Sam as the voice started laughing. Sam grabbed the phone.

"Who is this?" he demanded.

I heard a click as the caller hung up. I stared at Sam, unable to move; my whole body trembling. He wrapped his arms around me and I dissolved into tears.

"Pl -please... don't le-leave me, Sam. P-Please," I begged between sobs. Linda took the phone from him and hung it up while he steered me to the couch. She and Jackson moved to the kitchen.

"I'm not going anywhere, Janet. I am right here, my love. I'm right here." He spoke reassuringly. Suddenly, I could not breathe. I started gasping for air. "Janet, look at me," Sam ordered as his eyes locked on mine. "You are OK. Take a deep breath. It's OK. I am not going to let anybody hurt you. Chase!" he called out, his eyes still focused on mine. "Bring me one of those sacks the chips came in." She hurried from the kitchen with a white, lunch-size paper bag. "Here," he instructed me, "breathe into this." He held the sack over my nose and mouth. "That's right. Breathe deep. Slowly. That's good." When my breathing became slower and more controlled, he removed the bag, put his arms back around me and started singing quietly.

> "Sweet hour of prayer! Sweet hour of prayer!
> That calls me from a world of care,
> and bids me at my Father's throne
> make all my wants and wishes known.
> In seasons of distress and grief,
> my soul has often found relief,
> and oft escaped the tempter's snare
> by thy return, sweet hour of prayer!
>
> Sweet hour of prayer! Sweet hour of prayer!

116

The joys I feel, the bliss I share
of those whose anxious spirits burn
with strong desires for thy return!
With such I hasten to the place
where God my Savior shows his face,
and gladly take my station there,
and wait for thee, sweet hour of prayer!

Sweet hour of prayer! Sweet hour of prayer!
Thy wings shall my petition bear
to him whose truth and faithfulness
engage the waiting soul to bless.
And since he bids me seek his face,
believe his word, and trust his grace,
I'll cast on him my every care,
and wait for thee, sweet hour of prayer!" [6]

It took me a minute to realize where I was. The last thing I remembered was Sam's rich voice singing to me; filling me with peace. We were still sitting on the couch, his arms gently enfolding me. The lights were off.

"Sam?" I whispered.

"I'm here." He answered quietly.

"What time is it?"

"About four thirty."

"Where's Linda?"

"In your bed."

"I should go make her move over so you can at least lie down on the couch and get some sleep." I offered.

"I'm fine." He assured me. "I kind of like things the way they are."

I snuggled closer to his side. "Me, too."

---

[6] "Sweet Hour Of Prayer", William W. Walford, Public Domain

Chapter 32
Saturday, March 18

"Are you two going to sleep all day?" Linda was standing in front of the couch with her hands on her hips.

"What time is it?" I asked groggily.

"Seven fifteen, time to get up and get going." She replied with way too much enthusiasm for a Saturday morning.

Sam opened one eye, "Go home, Chase"

Jackson spoke up from inside the folds of his sleeping bag. "Yeah, Chase, can it. We don't need your noise."

I sat up straight and stretched. Sam stood up and groaned. "Ohhh, I am stiff!" He complained, twisting his body from side to side trying to loosen up. "Anybody want to go out for breakfast?" He suggested.

"Now you're talking." Jackson's head popped out the end of his bag.

"Sorry Jackson," Sam apologized. "You're not done. I want you here a few more days; at least until Monday for sure."

"Two more days?" I asked.

"Yes. I do not want to take any chances. His behavior this time hasn't fit with so much of what he has done previously. I'm just hoping he'll stick with the same time frame and since we have interrupted it, he'll quit... at least for this month." He explained.

"Fine," said Jackson. "Hope you don't choke on your bacon." He pulled his head back in the sleeping bag and turned over.

"We're supposed to be at the church this morning at nine thirty," I reminded Sam.

"Why are you going to church today?" Linda inquired. "It's Saturday."

"Our church is having its annual Spring Fling next weekend. Sam and I signed up to work the Rummage Sale. We have to start sorting through stuff today and getting it organized." I explained.

"Then we better get a move on if we're going to breakfast," Sam warned. "Potter's has a breakfast buffet on the weekend. They do a pretty decent job." He suggested.

"I'll eat some bacon for Jackson," Linda joked as we went through the serving line.

"Forget Jackson," Sam countered. "I'm eating bacon for myself!"

The line moved along quickly. There was everything breakfast a person could dream of eating. I got bacon, scrambled eggs, and biscuits with gravy. Milk and orange juice completed my selections. Sam had a pile of bacon, sausage links, and a stack of pancakes with coffee and orange juice for his first round. Linda went with a ham and cheese omelet with hash browns and toast to go with her coffee. When Sam went back to get a ham and cheese omelet and hash browns I asked him to bring me a sausage patty and a small bowl of grits. Linda finished up with a plate of fresh fruit. We were all so stuffed when we finished eating, we could hardly waddle out to our cars.

"Sam, don't bring me here again for breakfast." I moaned.

"You didn't like it?" He looked surprised.

"No, that's the problem. I loved it. I ate way too much. I am going to be really miserable all day."

"That's the problem with buffets," Linda added her opinion. "You feel obligated to eat more than you really need. See you guys tonight," she called as she got in her car and headed home.

There were about thirty boxes of various sizes at the church to go through for the rummage sale lined up at one end of the Fellowship Hall. Tables had been set up in a big "U" formation with the tables lined up against the two long, outer walls and across the far end of the room. Two additional long rows filled the space in the center of the room to accommodate all the donations.

"This is going to take a while!" Sam exclaimed as he set the first box on a table near the door that would probably be used as a check out area for customers. "Where do we put what?" He wondered aloud.

"How about if we put clothes on the left wall; we can start with baby stuff at this end and go down the wall with children's, teens, men's and women's. And maybe all the shoes going around the corner. Toys can go on the right side with household stuff on the right center row and tools and such on the left center row. We can put books on the back table. That at least gives us a place to start." I suggested. "We can make changes as we go."

"Sounds like a good plan to me. You start with that box and I'll take the next one." Sam approved my strategy as he lifted a second box onto the table.

Our designated content areas worked pretty well for the first ten or so boxes. Then we ran into some things that could be in more than one area. First was a set of small dishes that could be used by children in a play kitchen area. The set could also be used to feed a baby or young child; as well as small serving plates for cookies or finger food at a party. We also had some plastic storage boxes that could be used to store leftover food in the refrigerator or freezer. They could be used in the garage to store screws, nails, and what have you at a workbench or even to store fishing lures and tackle articles.

Sam got excited when he opened a box to find a toy chemistry set. "My brother and I used to have one of these," he reminisced. "About the only thing we made with any success were stink bombs. That awful smell would fill up the house and Mother would have to raise all the windows to air it out." He laughed at the memories. "One time, it was in the middle of winter, there was a big ice storm. Jeff and I got in the bedroom and made a big batch of the stuff. We nearly froze to death! All wrapped up in our coats and blankets while she opened the windows and doors until she got the stink out." He smiled at the images passing through his mind. "I think that was the last time we ever used it. Mother probably threw it away."

A few boxes later, I found an Easy-Bake Oven. "Patti had one of these! I loved to help her bake cookies and little cakes in it."

"You can really cook with that?"

"Oh, yeah. It uses a light bulb. They have little packages you mix up…lots of fun!"

"Is that how you learned to cook so well?" He stopped unpacking and looked at me with interest.

"Probably not," I laughed. "I used to do almost all the cooking for our family. Mom and Dad both worked when I was in high school. I got home before they did so I started cooking supper. Mother was a good cook. She would let me make the mashed potatoes when I was a kid… and cakes… we spent a lot of time in the kitchen when I was growing up." I remembered fondly.

The next box was full of books; children's books, cook books, comic books, How-To books, mystery books, romance, thrillers, every kind of book imaginable – almost. "I love books! I could take this whole box home with me." I said wistfully.

"Why do you like books so much?" Sam was curious.

"Because I love to read. And some day I want to be an author. I was in the Library Club in Junior High and High School. I even helped our church set up their library. I just love books." I shrugged.

Sam picked up one of the cookbooks and started thumbing through it. "Some of these sound good. Oh, here is one for Chicken and Dumplings. Do you know how to make that? My Mother made the best dumplings; I sure would like some soon," he hinted.

I laughed. "You're not too subtle are you? I can fix you some dumplings. I'll make you a big pot full next week while I'm on Spring Break." Sam grabbed me around the waist and swung me around.

"I love you, Janet Carter." He exclaimed teasingly.

"I love you too, Sam," I replied quietly.

He stopped short, set me down and looked at me intently. "Really?"

"Yes, really," I confirmed with a shy smile.

His blue eyes twinkled with excitement and his face lit up with a great big smile. He wrapped his arms around me and squeezed me tightly. He kissed my forehead, "That's the best thing I have ever heard."

"Sam, I need to breathe," I said with what little air I had in my lungs from his tight embrace. He loosened his grip and I continued. "And we need to get back to the boxes. We still have a third of them to unpack. I don't know if we'll have enough room for everything!" We turned to stare at the tables that were filling up quickly. "We can ask Pastor Jenkins if there are any more tables. Do you think we could fit another row in the center part?" I asked.

"It'll be a little crowded but I think we could do it." He guessed. "Maybe we can just squeeze stuff in a little closer. That would be easier than setting up more tables and moving things around."

"You're probably right." I concurred. "We can add some tables next week while we are pricing everything if we just have to have more space."

We finished the remaining boxes in just a little over two hours. It would have gone faster if we hadn't stopped to remember all the instances in our childhood some of the items brought to mind; the roller skates and banged up knees, the jigsaw puzzles put together on the table in the corner of the living room, the child-size rocking chair that was almost identical to the one stored in my parents attic, the wooden tool box that looked just like the one Sam's dad used. We shared laughter and special memories throughout the day.

Pastor Jenkins came in as we got the final items out of the last box. "Oh good, I caught you." He said cheerily. "My wife made some peanut butter cookies for you to snack on today and I am just now getting by to leave them for you. I guess you'll just have to take them with you." He suggested with a laugh. "My, you have gotten a lot done. This looks great," he added as he looked at the tables piled high with donated items.

"I can't believe we have been doing this all day," Sam announced as he looked at his watch and realized it was four twenty. Pastor Jenkins left to finish a few more errands before he could go home. He thanked us for our hard work and promised to see us in the morning.

"At least we got through it all," I applauded. "Mrs. Layne and I have to put a price on all this stuff next week. We are supposed to meet a couple of other women here Tuesday morning. Something tells me that she and I won't have near as much fun as we did today!" I mused. "It *has* been a good day, hasn't it?" Sam agreed. "Are you ready to go get something to eat? I could be hungry."

"After all I ate this morning I never thought I would be saying this but I think I could be too." I realized.

After a short discussion, we decided to go back to my apartment to let Molly out. From there we would call Linda to come over for bacon, lettuce and tomato sandwiches in honor of Jenkins. "Think you're up to another attempt at a game night?" Sam asked.

"I'm always ready to play games." I admitted enthusiastically.

Jackson sliced tomatoes while I cooked the bacon and Sam took Molly outside. "It will be nice to have a 'home cooked meal' for a change." He mused.

"It's just more sandwiches like you have been having." I noted sympathetically.

"What I have been having is cold left-overs from the fridge," He informed me.

"Why?"

"I can't make any noise or do anything that would let someone know I am here. So, I can't warm up food because they might smell it." He explained.

"What do you do all day? I figured you were at least watching television or listening to the radio or something."

"Nope, no noise. I play solitaire or read or take a nap." He counted on his fingers.

"I am so sorry," I sympathized.

"It's OK; comes with the territory. I get used to it," he admitted with resignation.

Linda arrived with a gallon of milk, a box of cereal, and a large bag of potato chips. "I figured you were running low on food for the human garbage disposal." She nodded at Jackson while putting the milk in the refrigerator and the cereal in the cabinet.

Sam came in just in time to hear Linda's comment. "Thanks Chase, that is right thoughtful of you," he teased as she put the chips on the table.

Sam had just finished saying grace when the telephone rang. I stopped breathing and looked at him. "I'll get it." He offered. "Hello. No one here by that name. That's OK." He hung up the receiver and returned to the table. "Wrong number," he squeezed my hand.

After two games of Scrabble and a plate of peanut butter cookies, we decided to call it a night. It had been a long day. I, for one, was ready to go to bed. Sam kissed me on top of the head and said his goodbyes.

Chapter 33
Sunday, March 19

I awoke to the delectable aroma of the ham I had put in the oven before I went to bed. I headed to the kitchen to check it and start peeling potatoes to make scalloped potatoes. Green beans and tomatoes would complete the meal. Everything should be ready to eat by the time we got home from church. Linda even decided to go with us so she could come back and eat lunch after church.

At the conclusion of an inspiring sermon on singing praises to the Lord and giving thanks for His protection, Pastor Jenkins thanked everyone for bringing donations for the rummage sale and reminded us that we still needed baked goods for the bake sale. After church, he informed Sam and me that six more boxes had come in before church this morning. After checking with her, Mrs. Layne and I agreed to come in early on Tuesday to get them unpacked.

Officer Jackson and Molly had become great friends during his stay at the apartment; she was sitting in his lap when we got home from church. "She's really good company. Maybe I should get a little dog to take with me on all my assignments," Jackson considered.

"Or not," said Sam as he got Molly's leash to take her outside while Linda and I finished getting everything ready for lunch.

"I have died and gone to heaven," Jackson exclaimed when he tasted the scalloped potatoes and ham. "And I've never had green beans and tomatoes mixed together before but these are really good, too!" he added.

"There goes any chance for leftovers to eat tomorrow," Sam complained with a chuckle. "I should have known better than to leave you here, Jackson."

"It's OK, Reynolds. There is still some ham in the kitchen," Linda informed him. She paused and then said, "I have an idea. Why don't you and Janet go for a drive? Go spend some private time together. Jackson and I will clean up here. I'll take Molly out later so stay as long as you want," She offered eagerly.

"That's the best idea you've had this year," Sam responded enthusiastically. "I'm not sticking around for you to change your mind. You ready to go?" He looked at me with a twinkle in his eye.

"I get the feeling that Linda was trying to get rid of us. Did it seem that way to you?" I questioned Sam after we had gotten in the car.

"You never know about Chase. She could have a thing for Jackson and wants some time to be alone with him or they could be plotting the next office rumors. I only know that she gave me the perfect opportunity to be alone with you. I don't have to be told twice; it's my favorite thing to do!" He responded candidly.

"We're not out of the woods yet, are we?" I asked as we drove.

"What do you mean?"

"Well, Mr. X didn't show up for me, even though his past behavior indicated that he would. But it doesn't mean Mrs. Layne is safe either." I explained my thinking.

"Unfortunately, you're right. She is our main focus for this week. I am somewhat surprised that she and the kids did not go on a little vacation for Spring Break. I know she said if she had a chance she would leave town." Sam mused aloud.

"She also said it was different because she has a family." I reminded him. "Are you going to move Jackson to her house?"

"Yes. He will be going over there Tuesday morning. He will be off tomorrow when he leaves your place. And then he will take up residence at the Layne household."

"Are we going where I think we're going?" I inquired with excitement.

"Could be," he winked and smiled mischievously as he turned off the main road onto the gravel one. Sam got a blanket from the trunk and we walked down the hill to the edge of the stream. The sun was warm and the air was chilly; it made for an interesting and pleasant mix.

I sat on the blanket. Sam stretched out beside me leaning back on one elbow. "How did you ever find this wonderful place?" I asked in awe of the peaceful surroundings; the birds singing in the trees and the stream babbling as it flowed past us.

"A buddy of mine used to lease this property for hunting." He answered.

"They don't hunt here anymore?"

"No, the new owner doesn't allow it."

"It's nice that they still let you come. They *do* let you come, right? I mean, we're not trespassing, are we?"

Sam laughed. "No, we're not trespassing. I have a question for you. When my friend first showed me this place, he asked if I were going to build a house, where would I put it. What would be your answer to that?" Sam raised his eyebrows questioningly.

Slowly I scanned the entire clearing giving serious thought to his challenge. "See over there where the trees sort of recede," I pointed to a spot across the stream. "I would put it in that little alcove."

"That's the same spot I picked. What kind of house would you put there?" he continued with interest.

"Something with big windows and a wide porch wrapped all the way around so you could sit outside in all kinds of weather and enjoy the stunning views of the woods." I described.

"That would be nice." He reflected. We sat in comfortable silence for a while; each deep in our own thoughts. Finally, Sam broke the stillness, "As much as I hate to say this, we probably should be going. It will be getting dark soon."

"OK, if you promise one thing," I responded.

"What's that?" he asked.

"Promise that we can come back here soon. I love it here!" I said earnestly.

"I'll tell you what. How about if we come back on Thursday? I will even pack a picnic lunch. We can come early and just spend the whole day." He offered.

"It's a deal! Are you sure you don't want me to make lunch?" I asked.

"Nope. I'm going to take care of everything," he said with a sparkle in his eye.

Chapter 34
Monday, March 20

I turned over and looked at the clock. Ten after eight. I wondered why Molly did not wake me up. She was not on her mat beside the bed. "Molly?" I called.

"She's in here with me." Linda answered from the living room. I put on my robe and headed that way.

"I can't believe I slept this late! She usually wakes me up before now to go out."

"She came in here when Reynolds got here about six and he took her out. He told Jackson to go on home and then he went to the station." Linda filled me in on the morning's events.

"Why didn't you wake me up?" I asked disappointedly.

"We decided you needed to get some rest. Besides, you are on Spring Break; you are supposed to sleep late. I told him I would stay until you got up" She explained. I went in the kitchen to get some coffee before coming back to sit on the couch. "You told him, didn't you?" She accused.

"Told who what?" I asked in confusion.

"Reynolds. How you feel about him." She stated bluntly. I blushed. "I knew it! I knew it! You must have told him Saturday because he was different yesterday."

"What are you talking about? What do you mean 'he was different yesterday'?" I questioned her remark.

"He has a whole new look of happiness…more than before. You probably didn't notice because you have it, too." She smiled knowingly.

"You *are* a hopeless romantic, aren't you?"

"No, I'm just observant," she defended.

"Why were you in such a hurry for us to leave yesterday afternoon?" I asked.

"Because I knew you would stay here and play games with me and Jackson to be polite when you really wanted to be alone. It does not take a genius to figure that out. Well, Jackson might be a little clueless," she laughed.

"Do you like Jackson?"

"Romantically? No. I was dating a guy but we broke up about four months ago. Therefore, I am just kind of laying low for a while. I have enjoyed watching the relationship between you and Reynolds develop. It's nice to see something good growing between two great people who deserve to be happy."

"Now you're getting mushy." I smiled. "What are you going to do this week? Are you supposed to stay with me?"

"I don't think so. I will be going in to the station after lunch. I guess I'll be back on patrol." We talked for a little while longer before she left.

I took a chicken out of the freezer, put it in a pot and covered it with water. I turned the burner on the stove to medium to cook it so I could make the chicken and dumplings I had promised Sam. "It's quiet here with just the two of us, isn't it girl?" I remarked to Molly who was sitting by her water bowl watching me. The doorbell rang. I opened the door as far as the chain would allow. A young man was standing there with a beautiful arrangement of spring flowers.

"Delivery for Janet Carter," He announced.

"Who are they from?" I was more than a little apprehensive.

"I don't know ma'am. They just tell me where to take them. There's a card."

'OK. Let me see it." He handed me the card through the narrow opening. My heart swelled when I read it. "Thank you for bringing springtime to my life. I love you, Sam" I opened the door and took the flowers. "Oh, Molly just look! Aren't they lovely?" I set them on the table and went to the phone.

The dispatcher informed me that "Chief Reynolds is in a meeting." I declined to leave a message and returned to the kitchen. I made a quick inventory of the cabinets and refrigerator and wrote out a list of things I needed from the grocery store. I turned the chicken pot down to low, secured Molly in the kitchen and headed out. It was a beautiful day. The sun was shining brightly and bringing welcome warmth to the cool morning air. The red birds were singing sweet melodies from where they perched in the branches and the squirrels twitched their bushy tails as they chased each other, scampering from tree to tree.

I was in the middle of making an apple pie when the telephone rang. "Hello?" I wiped my hands on the kitchen towel while cradling the handset between my ear and my shoulder.

"Hi, how is your day going? Beckett said you called earlier." Sam's strong, cheerful voice was music to my ears.

"I just wanted to say thank you for the beautiful flowers. Molly and I love them," I said sincerely. "Are you coming over for lunch?" I inquired. "I'll make you a ham sandwich."

"Sounds like an offer I can't refuse," he teased. "I'll be there in about an hour and a half. I have some information you might be interested in hearing."

"And you're not going to give me any clues about what that might be, are you?"

"Nope," he laughed. "See you in a little while."

I swept and mopped the kitchen and vacuumed the rest of the apartment. The chicken was cooling so I could debone it and I had just taken the apple pie out of the oven when Sam finally arrived. I gave him a big hug and thanked him again for the flowers.

"They look good," he observed favorably. "I was hoping they would be colorful."

I put our sandwiches on the table. Sam's eyes lit up when I set a small bowl of scalloped potatoes near his plate. "There was a little bit left over. I thought you might want them."

"You thought right!" He smiled delightedly.

As soon as he finished saying grace I asked, "So what's your big news?"

"We got word this morning that there was a murder over in Big Mound. Apparently, a woman was strangled last Friday night." Sam watched me closely. "She was a teacher."

"What!" I gasped.

"She and her husband had gone out to celebrate her birthday, which was Saturday, and then he left to go camping with the Boy Scout Troup he works with. He found her when he got home yesterday afternoon."

"Do you think it was Mr. X?" I asked incredulously.

"Well, it seems that way. I have been in touch with them and they want me to come look over the evidence. I am going tomorrow since you will be busy with Mrs. Layne at church. I'll leave early in the morning and should be back before dark."

"I hope it *was* him and he has moved somewhere else to do his killing." I responded vehemently. "Oh, I'm sorry, that sounds awful." I recoiled at my own outburst. "I didn't mean it that way. I do not want him to keep going. I do not want anyone to have to go through what we have been through this past month. I want him to get caught." I added with frustration.

Sam squeezed my hand. "I understand what you mean. I want him caught, too. Let's just hope his last minute change in plans caused him to leave some clear evidence as to who he is and where we can find him. Not to change the subject but, didn't I smell apple pie when I came in?" He added with a clever smile.

"Yes you did and it's for supper." I informed him.

"I promise to eat some of it then but it sure would taste good right now while it's still warm." He looked at me with pleading eyes.

"You are bad, Sam Reynolds." I laughed as I got up and went in the kitchen.

He came up behind me while I was cutting the pie and put his arms around my waist. I leaned back against him; relishing the feeling of his strength and protection. "What are you going to do with the chicken?" he asked.

"I'm going to make dumplings. I promised you I would." His arms tightened their hold and he kissed my neck. "You're not going to have pie *or* dumplings if you don't go sit back down." I threatened. He retreated to the table.

Chapter 35
Tuesday, March 21

Tuesday morning dawned with a foggy drizzle. I worried about Sam making the two and a half hour drive to Big Mound and prayed for his safe return. Pastor Jenkins was unlocking the door of the church when I arrived. Mrs. Layne pulled in right beside me.

"What a dreary day for getting out!" Pastor Jenkins announced as we shook the moisture off our umbrellas and wiped our feet on the mat just inside the door.

"This is the kind of day for staying home and reading a good book," Mrs. Layne expressed her opinion as we walked to the Fellowship Hall. The boxes were waiting for us. "Where are we going to put any more stuff?" Mrs. Layne exclaimed as she surveyed the room of tables already heavily loaded.

"Good question," I remarked. "Most of that is clothes. I hope that when the other women are here and start marking prices, things can be folded and arranged a little neater so everything will fit better. But you know as soon as people start going through stuff it will just be a big mess again." I predicted.

We started unpacking. The boxes proved to contain more clothes, toys and books. The third box caused me to jump when I opened it. Lying on the top was a lime green tablecloth. "I have come to hate this color. It has nothing but appalling memories for me now."

"I couldn't agree with you more. I have taken everything that color out of my house and thrown it away." Mrs. Layne confessed.

"Has Officer Jackson started staying at your house yet?" I asked.

"He is supposed to come sometime today. Mark was not keen on having someone in the house but he finally relented after Detective Reynolds talked to him. I'm sort of glad… makes me feel a little safer to know he is close and available if something happens." She shared.

"I know what you mean. It was a little weird at first but I *did* sleep better because he and Linda were there." I admitted. "Did you hear about the murder in Big Mound? Sam says they think Mr. X did it."

"Really?" Mrs. Layne's eyes widened in surprised.

"Yeah, last Friday night, a teacher in Big Mound was strangled. Her birthday was Saturday!" I conveyed my newly gained knowledge.

"Oh, that would be a big relief if he has moved on." She agreed seriously.

"Sam went there today to look at their evidence and give them some assistance with it. He is supposed to be back before dark. I just hope this weather doesn't cause him any problems." We finished unpacking the last three boxes and joined the women who had come in to mark prices on each item. We stopped for the day about three thirty and I headed home to take Molly out. The fog had cleared up but the drizzle was still fairly steady.

I put the leftover chicken and dumplings, fried okra and cornbread in the oven to keep it warm until Sam arrived. I was more than a little concerned about how late it was getting. My imagination was working overtime, thinking of all the things that could have gone wrong. However, there was nothing I could do but wait and pray. It was well after dark before he made it back.

"I got stuck behind a really slow moving log truck. I know he was trying to be safe but I sure did wish he would speed up a bit. I was more than ready to be home. The roads between here and Big Mound are too winding to take any chances on passing in this kind of weather so I just had to bide my time." Sam explained when he finally made it to my apartment.

"I'm just glad you're here. I was really worried." I hugged him tightly; he kissed my forehead. "I hope you don't mind leftovers. I didn't think you would want to go out after that long drive."

"Not a problem for me! I would rather eat your leftovers than go out any day. I am starving. Can I help you do something?"

"Sure, I just have to set everything out of the oven. You grab the plates and we will be all set." I instructed.

While we ate, Sam recounted his trip to Big Mound. "The weather really slowed me down. It took a little over three hours to make it there. It was nasty driving. Then after I arrived and got situated in their conference room, I talked to the Officers on the case and reviewed the evidence they had gathered. It strongly indicates Mr. X is responsible. There are just two things that were not at the crime scene. There were no flowers and no card. That bothers me some but everything else was pretty much identical to our cases here." He related seriously.

"I decided to put in a call to Lakin Florist to get a little more information from them. For the three original murders, the flowers were ordered by phone the morning of the murders and picked up in the

132

afternoon. There were no flowers ordered last Friday. So, apparently he knew he wasn't coming here." He noted. "It may be that because he had to make last minute changes regarding his victim that he didn't bother with flowers this time."

"So you think Mrs. Layne is safe?" I asked hopefully.

"All things considered, I would say yes. But, just to play it safe, I'm going to leave Jackson there until Saturday." Sam informed me.

"Will you be going back to Big Mound?"

"Not unless they call me for some reason." He speculated. "Are you going to church tomorrow? Or did you get everything finished today?"

"There's still a little pricing to do but the other ladies can handle it so I guess I will be staying home. I'm thinking about taking Molly to the park."

"I can't go with you tomorrow; my desk is piled high with reports to complete." He informed me sadly. "But don't forget that Thursday we're going to the property and she will have a lot more room to run around." He reminded me enthusiastically.

I smiled at his excitement about our picnic on Thursday. "And you are still planning to bring our lunch? Right?"

"Absolutely! I have the menu all planned." He beamed.

"I can't wait to see what you come up with," I teased.

"You just wait, Missy. You'll be downright surprised." He smiled smugly.

Chapter 36
Wednesday, March 22

I was relieved to see the rain had stopped when I took Molly for her morning outing. Since the drizzle had been light and steady yesterday, the ground was soft but not muddy. The sun was clearing away the few clouds that remained. It was going to be a nice day. Molly and I stayed out for a while. After she got tired of catching the ball, I sat and watched while she chased the birds that were searching for worms in the soft earth. I knew it was time to go back inside when she finally came over and laid down beside the bench.

I was in a mood to bake so I spent the remainder of the morning in the kitchen making a batch of chocolate chip cookies, a pan of chocolate brownies, and a pan of blonde brownies. I decided to surprise Sam and take a plate of goodies to put in the break room at the station. I wrote a card of thanks for everyone's efforts on my behalf during the past several weeks to put with it.

Much to my disappointment Sam was not there when I arrived. "He had some business to take care of away from the station," the Desk Clerk informed me. She graciously accepted the cookies and brownies and promised to put them where everyone could enjoy them.

Molly and I headed to Lakin Park. We were greeted by Jack and Toby. "Hi Miss Carter," they called as they came running from across the playground. "Can we play with Molly?"

"Yes, as long as you keep her with you. Don't let anybody else have her," I instructed.

"Yes, ma'am," they agreed as they ran off toward the slide with Molly following close behind. I settled on the picnic table bench under a green top and started reading the book I had brought with me. I glanced up often to keep tabs on Molly and the boys.

"Reynolds said he thought you would be here," Linda walked up to the table. "Thanks for the brownies. They were delicious!" It was strange to see her in her uniform.

"Sam sent you here to check up on me, didn't he?" I accused.

She smiled. "Not 'check up' on you, just make sure you are OK. He's just being cautious."

"Well, you can let him know that I am just fine. Molly and I are enjoying the fresh air and sunshine." I said cheerily. His concern made me feel warm all over. "What are you doing this week? Staying busy?" I asked.

"Pretty much. I would have to admit, it is not as exciting as spending the day in your classroom but I like it. Didn't realize I missed it until I started back. You know, like the 'regulars' I see every day; old Mr. Vernon sitting on his porch waving as I drive by or Beverly, the cashier at the gas station where I stop to get a soda in the afternoon, Mrs. Findley out walking her dog. It's nice to have connections with the community." She looked happy as she shared the bright spots in her day. We talked for a little longer before we decided it was time for us both to leave. She returned to her squad car and I gathered Molly and my book and headed home.

I cooked a pan of green chili enchiladas in addition to a cheesy hominy casserole for supper. I left it warming in the oven until Sam arrived. "That smells wonderful!" He hugged me hello. "I hope you kept some of those chocolate chip cookies here." He smiled. "That was really sweet of you to bring all of that to the station. Everyone really appreciated it. I'm just sorry I missed you."

"Yeah, me too. You really did not need to send Linda to check on me. Molly and I were just enjoying the sun."

He looked sheepish, "I didn't do it just for you; she was my way of spending some time with you when I couldn't be there."

"Thank you, Sam," I smiled quietly, warmed by his thoughtfulness. "It was nice."

I set the food on the table while Sam took Molly outside. When they returned Sam informed me, "Molly wanted me to ask you something."

"Oh, she did? What does she want to know?" I chuckled in response.

"She was wondering if you had any more of those brownies left to take on our picnic tomorrow." He fidgeted with her leash.

"Actually, I do. Does she want the chocolate ones or the blonde ones?" I asked.

"Oh, I think she wants some of both kinds," he answered for her. I just laughed.

"Let's eat before everything gets cold." I encouraged.

"I can honestly say I have never had green chili enchiladas or the hominy stuff either." Sam stated. "But they are both really good! I was not expecting them to be as flavorful as they were. They are *almost* better than The Green Sombrero." He added with a teasing wink.

"You *must* like them," I noted. "You've only had three helpings. You're not going to have any room for cookies." I warned him.

"I *always* have room for cookies." He quipped. "I just might wait until later to eat them with a glass of milk." He decided as he patted his stomach and let out a big sigh. "Do you want to go for a ride or take in a movie?" He inquired.

"We can do whatever you would like to do. You seem a little antsy tonight." I noted with concern. "Is everything alright? Did you have a hard day at work?"

"Sorry, I just have a lot on my mind. Too many things vying for my attention." He explained with a strange look on his face. "There are a few things I need to get settled." He added mysteriously. "Maybe it would be best if I go on home." He stood up to leave. When I walked with him to the door, he held me tightly for several minutes before whispering in my ear, "Oh, Janet, I love you so much." He released me suddenly and said stiffly, "I'll see you tomorrow about ten." And he was out the door.

I turned in confusion and looked at Molly who was sitting by the table watching me. "What just happened?" I asked her. "Did I do or say something to upset him? Or is there something he knows that he doesn't want to tell me?" I shook my head in bewilderment.

Chapter 37
Thursday, March 23

I Did not sleep well and was not ready for the alarm to go off at seven. I tossed and turned all night thinking about Sam; curious and concerned about what was going on with him. Molly and I were waiting, brownies wrapped in foil and placed in a bag, when he arrived at ten.

"How are my ladies doing this morning?" He asked in a little too exuberant voice. "Are you ready to go?" I nodded and handed him the bag.

"Molly said you were supposed to carry these for her," I smiled.

He laughed. "Anything for you, my dear," he bowed and nodded at her.

The ride to the property was uncomfortably quiet. Sam seemed lost in thought, a thousand miles away. My heart beat increased and fear stirred in my being. When we arrived at the top of the hill Sam got out the blanket, a picnic basket and a thick cardboard tube. I sat on the rock by the stream and watched as he spread the blanket and put the basket and cardboard tube on one corner.

He turned to me and offered his hand. "May I have this dance?" he smiled with a twinkle in his eye. He started singing "If My Heart Had Windows" and we danced slowly to the rhythm of the song; his rich voice filling the meadow with beautiful music. When he had finished singing, he put his arms around my waist and looked deep into my eyes. "I know we only met a short time ago, but I feel I have known you forever. I honestly believe God has ordained you to be the woman to share my life. I want to be with you always, to hold you, to help you, to comfort you, to love you through whatever may come our way. I love you with all of my heart." As he knelt down on one knee he reached in his pocket and pulled out a small, navy blue, velvet covered box. "Will you do me the honor of becoming my wife? Will you marry me?" His vivid blue eyes were full of hope and love as he searched my face.

My heart stood still. I could not believe my greatest dream was coming true. God was truly giving me the desire of my heart. "Yes... YES!

Of course I'll marry you!" I threw my arms around his neck. "I love you, Sam."

I felt the tenseness leave his body as he held me close. He let out a big sigh of relief, "I was so afraid you would say no." He confided as he kissed me tenderly.

Molly started barking excitedly and jumping around us. We laughed as we watched her antics. "I think she knows that something very special just happened," I whispered; my heart bursting with joy.

We sat down on the blanket, Sam took the ring out of the box, and I saw it for the first time. My eyes widened and I gasped, "Oh Sam, it's beautiful!" Tears filled my eyes and slipped down my cheeks. "I can't believe this is really happening." The one karat, cushion cut diamond framed by smaller round diamonds was mounted on a twenty-four karat gold band. The dazzling stones sparkled brilliantly. He slipped it on my finger and I stared at it in amazement. "I don't deserve anything this magnificent."

He cupped my face with both his hands and our eyes locked. "Yes, you do," he smiled lovingly as he leaned over to kiss me.

My heart was beating so hard I thought it was going to jump out of my chest. "If this is a dream, please don't let me wake up."

"Oh, this is no dream, my dear. No dream at all." He beamed adoringly. "You have made me the happiest man alive!"

I sat there watching him beaming and humming. I was so taken by surprise that I was speechless. Sam laughed, "I don't think I have ever seen you at a loss for words."

"I don't know what to say. You caught me completely off guard! I think I'm in shock." I smiled. "So what do we do now?"

"What do you mean?" He asked hesitantly.

"This has never happened to me. I don't know what to do now," I explained shrugging my shoulders.

"Well," he smiled patiently. "I've never done this either but I think now we set a date and plan a wedding. Is there anything personal you want to ask me? You already know I have one brother. My favorite color is blue." He grinned mischievously.

"Sam Reynolds!" I thumped him on the arm. "You have been talking to Patti!"

"Yes, I did," he laughed. "And in all fairness, I am going to let you tell your version of the story."

"I don't believe this!" I shook my head. "When I was in college, before my parents got sick, there was a guy I kind of liked. I did not have any experience with dating or boyfriends, so I *confided* in my little sister, who

138

was a junior in High School at the time. I asked her for advice about how to let him know that I liked him. She told me to talk to him about something personal. I said 'You mean like how many brothers and sisters he has or what's his favorite color?' She has never let me live that down. OK, I will admit...I am way past naive... I am absolutely clueless when it comes to men and romance." I shared. "Linda kept telling me that you liked me but I thought it was just her imagination. I was afraid to let myself believe it could be true. Now, knowing my deepest, darkest secret, are you sure you don't want your ring back?"

He threw his head back and burst out laughing, "Not on your life! I love you even more." He hugged me until he stopped laughing. "I'm ready for some lunch; how about you?" He reached for the picnic basket.

"I can't wait to see what you fixed us to eat." I replied eagerly.

"It's an old family recipe," he whispered confidentially. "I had to check with my Mother to make sure it was OK to make it for you." He scanned the area to make sure no one was around. With a flourish, he pulled out a baggie containing a peanut butter and strawberry preserves sandwich and put it on my plate. "I even cut it corner to corner for you," he boasted proudly. It was my turn to laugh. Sam joined in and reminded me, "I told you I could make a mean sandwich."

"So you did. What did you bring to drink?" I asked. He pulled out two plastic glasses and a quart of milk. "You thought of everything, didn't you?" He held up a finger, reached back in the basket and got out a baggie of dog treats.

"Now, we all have something to eat." He smiled. "So, when do you want to get married? I'm guessing next week is a little too soon."

"Uh, yeah!" I gave him a "you've got to be kidding" look. "I don't know; after school is out, of course. When do you think is a good time?"

"I'm thinking three, maybe four months from now. Whenever the house is finished."

"House, what house?" I asked in confusion.

He reached around and picked up the cardboard tube, "The house we are going to build right over there." He pointed to the alcove in the trees we had discussed during our last visit to the property.

"What?" I shook my head in confusion.

"Here, look at these." He unrolled three sheets of blueprints and spread them out in front of us. "They all have wrap-around porches and lots of windows. Which one do you like best?"

"Sam? What are you saying?"

"This is my property... *our* property," He added, hardly able to contain his excitement as he spread his arms out wide to encompass the scenery around us.

"I *must* be dreaming. The most wonderful man I have ever known has just asked me to be his wife and now he is telling me that we are going to live in this beautiful place. Please God, don't let me wake up!" I addressed the sky. "This is a fairytale come true."

"And you are the princess," he added as he took my hand and kissed it. "This one is my favorite." He specified the plans on the far left. "I had them put in a library so you can have a room full of books and a desk for writing." He indicated a room with a bay window at the front of the house that would have a view of the meadow.

"How long have you been planning this?"

"Sort of since the day we met, but mostly since last Saturday."

"You did all of this in four days?" I asked in amazement. "No wonder you seemed a little distracted. They all have four bedrooms in addition to a master bedroom. How many kids do you want?" I asked studying the floor plans.

"As many as God will give us." He spoke reverently. "How many do *you* want?"

"I have always said I wanted four boys. Girls fight too much and they never let it go. Boys fight and it is done with. But I will be perfectly happy with whatever kind and however many God gives us; I just want them to be healthy."

We spent the rest of the afternoon discussing the pros and cons of each house plan and finally agreed on the one that was Sam's favorite. It did indeed have the best arrangement. "They'll start work on it next week." He informed me while munching on a brownie.

We picked the fifteenth of July for the wedding because Sam figured the house would be finished by then and would be ready for us to move in when we got back from our honeymoon. We talked about groomsmen and bridesmaids and how we wanted a small personal ceremony. By the time we were ready to head back to town, we had almost everything planned. I still felt like I was in the most wonderful dream I could ever have imagined. My life had completely changed in the short span of a few hours.

Sam sang to me on the way home; I snuggled close to him and thanked God for the blessings He had bestowed on me.

Chapter 38
Friday, March 24

Linda was coming up the stairs as Molly and I were leaving the apartment to go out back. "Let me see it!" She demanded. "Not too shabby!" she exclaimed as I thrust my hand out for her to look. "It's beautiful, congratulations. I knew it was coming; just did not know exactly when. I was off by two days. Hicks won the pot." She turned and followed us down the stairs.

"You were betting on when Sam would propose?" I asked in astonishment.

"Of course! When's the wedding?"

"Why? Are y'all betting on that, too?" I laughed.

"No, I just wanted to know." She admitted seriously.

"July fifteenth. I do not know what time yet. We have to talk to Pastor Jenkins first. Will you be one of my bridesmaids?" I asked as we sat on the bench and I unleashed Molly to run around.

"Are you serious?" Linda looked truly pleased. "I would love to! Thanks for asking me. Sure Reynolds won't mind?" She joked.

"Of course not." I replied. We discussed all those kinds of details yesterday. I still cannot believe this is really happening. I could not sleep last night. I kept pinching myself to make sure I was awake and not dreaming." I beamed in excitement.

"You know Randy is going to be mad," Linda chuckled.

"I thought about that. I told Sam he'll have to ask his permission." I joined in her laughter.

We talked for a few more minutes before she had to return to work. Molly and I followed her back to the patrol car. "Are you going to be at school next week?" I asked.

"Yes, Reynolds said I could come say bye to the kids. I think I will be there all week. He is leaving everyone where they are just to be on the safe side."

"I bet everybody will be glad when they can get back to their normal work schedules." I remarked.

"It's been interesting, to say the least." She responded honestly.

I had just finished putting a Frito chili pie in the oven when someone knocked on the door. Molly was barking and jumping with excitement. I peeked through the narrow opening half expecting to see Sam, early for lunch. Instead I was greeted by a stunning bouquet of red roses.

"Delivery for Janet Carter," the deliveryman said.

I took the latch off the door and accepted the gorgeous floral arrangement. The card read "To the future Mrs. Reynolds, Thank you for making me the happiest man alive. Love, Sam." For the next forty-five minutes I could only smile and giggle to myself. I felt so blessed I could hardly contain my joy. God loved me so much that He sent a wonderful man to share the rest of my life. When Sam finally showed up for lunch, I gave him a big hug. "You are too good to me Sam. They are beautiful! Thank you so much."

"You are more than welcome," he laughed. "But all the thanks go to you! What smells so good?" He hugged me back.

"Frito pie," I told him. "I thought you might like something warm since it's a little chilly today."

"You are all I need to keep warm," he winked.

"OK, let's not get carried away, Shakespeare," I laughed and poked him in the stomach. "Have a seat. I'll have it right out."

"How has your morning been?" He asked cheerfully as he blew on the bite of Frito pie to cool it a bit.

"Linda stopped by for a little while and I got roses. This has been a wonderful day, so far," I smiled. "What have you been doing?"

"I talked to the Chief in Big Mound," he said cautiously.

"And what did he have to say?" I asked with a slight feeling of trepidation.

"There seems to be a bit of discrepancy in the husband's alibi. The time frame he gave them doesn't exactly match up with the one from the Scout Master he went camping with."

"How so?"

"He first said he left the restaurant about eight fifteen, after having dinner with his wife, and went straight to the camp out; which is a thirty minute drive. When the officers checked with the Scout Master, he said the husband did not arrive until around nine thirty. So they went back to the husband and he said he stopped by the store to get some things they needed for the next day." Sam explained.

The Birthday Killer

"So-o-o, how does that affect the Mr. X theory?" I asked uneasily.

"It doesn't, just yet. They are doing more follow up and will keep me informed as to what turns up. It is just professional courtesy. They know I have an interest in the case." He reached over and took my hand. "Everything is OK." He assured me.

"Do you want some cookies?" I asked, changing the subject.

Chapter 39
Saturday, March 25

I had spent Friday afternoon cooking for the bake sale. I made four pies, two apple and two chocolate chess, a strawberry cake and three dozen peanut butter cookies. Sam helped me carry them to the booth set up just outside the Fellowship Hall. "I don't know why we couldn't just leave all these at home. I will be glad to pay for them. We could put them in the freezer and then have some whenever we want." He reasoned.

"I think I will be able to make you a pie whenever you want one." I scolded him. "Besides, I don't have room in my little freezer for all of these." I laughed at the sad face he was trying to make.

We took our places at the cashier's spot for the rummage sale a few minutes before everything got started. When the bell rang, people came streaming in to peruse all the bargains. One of the first items purchased was the lime green tablecloth. I flinched when the woman put it on the table with her other items. "That just gives me the creeps," I confided to Sam. "Every time I see that color I feel sick."

"I promise not to allow anything that color in our house." He smiled solemnly giving me a quick hug between customers.

Mrs. Layne came to join us. "Sorry, I'm running late this morning. Mark Junior managed to get himself locked in the bathroom and I didn't think we would ever get that door open!" She apologized.

"Ah, the joys of parenthood," Sam laughed. "I can't wait."

We quickly figured out a system to check people out that made the line go smoothly. Mrs. Layne added the price of each item, I took the money and Sam bagged it. Every once in a while we would have a slight lull and we could catch our breath. Mrs. Layne admired my ring making pleasant noises as she checked it out.

Sam and Mrs. Layne greeted people they knew as they came in to shop. Short conversations ensued during the checkout process. Linda came in right before lunch with a couple of guys from the station. "Finally, someone *I* know," I sighed with relief. We all laughed.

"You guys are busy!" Linda noted. "There's a huge crowd outside at the other booths so you're probably not done in here. It was hard finding a place to park."

"We've had a steady flow of customers all morning." I informed her. "And look at the tables; they're still full!" I scanned the room in amazement. "It doesn't look like anything is gone and yet, we have sold a ton of stuff."

A group of kids from another church walked in the door; wearing lime green t-shirts sporting their church logo. Mrs. Layne groaned. "I think if I see one more person with lime green on, I am going to scream!"

"I didn't realize it was such a popular color." I observed. "If I never see it again, it will be too soon."

"Why don't you two take a break while there's a lull? Chase can stay here and help me run things." Sam suggested.

"That sounds like a great idea," Mrs. Layne said hastily. "Let's go," she grabbed my arm and pulled. "I want to see what there is to eat."

"I'll take whatever you bring back for me," Sam called after us as we made our exit.

The church lawn was as busy as an anthill that had just been disturbed. The various booths hosted by different Sunday school classes offered a wide array of activities for every age group. There was face painting, a ring toss game, a fishing game, pick a duck, spin the wheel, basketball throw, pop the balloon dart game, make a necklace, horseshoes, and a cake walk to name a few. We headed to the snack booth where they were selling popcorn, nachos, chips, corndogs and hot dogs. I bought two hot dogs and an order of nachos for Sam and a corndog for myself. Mrs. Layne got a hot dog and a bag of chips. Mr. Nicholas came up to the snack booth as we were leaving. He was wearing a black suit and sporting a lime green tie. I cringed.

"Good afternoon, ladies." He smiled. "I see you made it through the week. Glad you are still with us. I always enjoy coming to this every year. It is good to see everyone having such a good time. Wish I could stay longer but I am on the way to my niece's wedding." He informed us pointing to his tie.

We headed back inside to eat. Sam devoured his hotdogs and nachos and then took his turn to go outside for a break. "I'll bet you a soda he buys more food," Linda laughed.

"I'm not taking that bet! You are probably right!" I laughed in agreement with her.

When Sam returned about twenty minutes later Linda asked, "What did you eat Reynolds?"

"I just had a couple of corndogs and talked with Mr. Nicholas." He replied. Linda nodded her head and smiled at me.

"Please tell me you don't have a lime green tie," I looked at Sam pleadingly and shuddered at the thought.

He put his arms around me, "No I don't but if I did I would have already gotten rid of it. I wouldn't do that to you." He promised with a squeeze.

While we stayed busy during the afternoon, the crowds did not overwhelm us like they had in the morning. The women who had helped mark stuff earlier in the week showed up to start boxing up the leftovers around five thirty. We had sold about two-thirds of what we had; the remaining items would be donated to Goodwill.

"We *are* going out to eat tonight, aren't we?" I asked tiredly. "Either that or Molly will have to fix something for us," I teased.

"Of course! I wouldn't ask you to cook for me after the long day we've had," Sam commented. "Besides, if I don't start showing up at some of my places, I am going to lose my 'regular' status. Can't have that happen!" He grinned. "Where do you want to go?"

"Surprise me. It really doesn't matter as long as I don't have to fix it!" I replied. "Whatever you want is fine with me." We drove to the Burger Barn; Sam wanted a malt.

Chapter 40
Monday, March 27

Linda was waiting at her usual place by the front door when Sam dropped me off Monday morning. "What was the final tally for Saturday?" she asked as we walked to the room.

"Pastor Jenkins announced yesterday that we made over thirty-two hundred dollars. I'd say the day was fairly successful." I replied.

The kids were excited to be back at school. They all had stories to share about what they had done during Spring Break. I was surprised, and pleased, that they had no problems jumping back into the routine we had before the break. "I really expected to have some behavior issues with them being out for a whole week," I shared with Linda. "I think they must have missed the security of the structure we have in the room. They really seem very settled."

Sam came at lunchtime bearing four large boxes of pizza. "I figured I better bring a peace offering to butter Randy up before I ask for your hand in marriage." He joked.

"Probably a good idea," I quipped.

Linda spoke up, "I don't know if it will help you out or not, Reynolds. He's a pretty tough character!" We all laughed and the kids were excited about the pizza. It appeared that Sam and Randy were having a race to see who could eat the most. They were both up to five pieces when Mrs. Post entered the room toting a half a dozen lime green, helium filled balloons.

I gasped, "No, no, no!" Every muscle in my body tensed.

Sam jumped up. "I'll take those, Mrs. Post." He was out the door and gone in a flash leaving Mrs. Post standing there looking guilty.

"I'm so sorry; I wasn't thinking. Can you forgive me?" she pleaded.

"It's OK, Mrs. Post." Linda consoled her. "We were just hoping this was all over since we haven't heard anything from him in over a week."

Mrs. Post left the room and Linda turned her attention to me. My heart was racing and my body shaking; Linda put her hand on my shoulder.

"It's OK. Reynolds will take care of it. Do you need some alone time to get yourself together? I can take the kids out for a while. Or would you rather go out yourself?" She suggested the available options.

"I think I'll leave the room for a little while. Thank you, Linda; I'm so glad you're here." My mind was reeling in shock and confusion but as I headed to the door, I was aware of Linda asking who wanted more pizza. She knew how to refocus them. I sat outside on the porch steps near my room. I was too numb to cry. My mind was racing with muddled questions. After a while, Sam came out and sat with me.

"Are you OK?" He asked quietly as he put his arms around me.

"Why is this still happening? I mean, all our birthdays are past. He killed the teacher in Big Mound. This should be over, Sam. I can't go on this way." My words tumbled over each other as I expressed my frustration, confusion, and fear.

"I can answer some of those questions...sort of," he paused before completing his explanation. "The balloons were ordered three weeks ago; before anybody's birthday. Order came in the mail with money; just like with the plants. Only this time, all three of you got balloons. Mrs. Martinez's school sent them back since she is not there. The note with the balloons said 'If you are getting these...you have another birthdate to look forward to'."

I pulled away to look at him. "Why did he send them to me? By all accounts, I was the intended victim. It doesn't make any sense." I questioned.

"Pure speculation on my part, but maybe in case someone made the connection and reported the order to the authorities it wouldn't be obvious who was supposed to be the victim." He explained his theory. "And...," he continued cautiously. "We aren't one hundred percent sure that he killed the teacher in Big Mound. That is still under investigation. Nevertheless, on a more positive note; we have not had any direct contact from him in over a week. Maybe the balloons, again I'm just speculating, are his way of saying it is over."

"Oh Sam," I leaned back into his arms and put my head on his shoulder. "I hope you're right."

Chapter 41
Friday, March 31

The rest of week passed quickly and uneventfully. The children started the morning off telling Linda that they were going to miss her. It was hard to believe it was her last day with us. She had become a fixture in the classroom and I had come to depend on her ability to quickly size up the situation and step in to avert disaster. The kids always responded to her in such a positive way.

It was getting close to lunch when Sam, who had promised to bring pizza, arrived as always, right on time. The kids quickly sat on the rug with the paper plates I passed out to hold their pizza. We joined them on the floor and started eating.

"Y'all are being so solemn. I feel like this is my last meal or something." Linda announced. "Come on, guys; lighten up. I'll come back to visit every now and then." All the kids clapped their hands and cheered.

"We hope you will come back often," I invited. "I'm going to have to learn how to teach by myself again. I don't mean to get maudlin but I really have enjoyed you being here. You have helped in so many ways. I could not have gotten through this past month without you. Thank you, Linda."

"Hey," Sam interjected. "You two sound like you're moving across the country from each other. You'll be seeing her all the time," he reminded me. "She *is* going to be in the wedding, isn't she?"

Linda and I looked at each other and laughed. "Men!" Linda exclaimed. "They just don't get it!" Sam shrugged.

It was such a nice day we decided to take the kids outside to play instead of laying down for a nap. "See you after school." Sam said as he left to go back to work while we lined up and got ready to go out. Linda and I stood under the trees on the edge of the playground and watched while the children scattered. Randy, Tim, and Ronnie went for the monkey bars while Donna, Tina and Toni chose the swings. Dave and Curtis climbed to the top of the slide and zoomed to the bottom only to run around and start the process over again.

"I am definitely going to miss these guys," Linda sighed. "It's amazing how quickly you can get attached to them."

"Yes, it certainly is! I cannot imagine teaching anywhere else but here. I feel so blessed to be able to share in their lives." I agreed. "Do you think I'm crazy to have the kids in the wedding?"

"No, I think it's kind of special. I am really looking forward to it. I can't wait to see Randy walking you down the aisle." She replied enthusiastically. "Now, are you and Reynolds doing house stuff or wedding stuff tomorrow?"

"House stuff. We're going someplace in Dallas to pick out flooring and counter tops and whatever else is on the list Sam got from the builder, Mr. Morgan. He says 'they have the best products at the lowest prices'. I figure he gets a kickback for sending people there. But that's OK…it will be a fun trip. What are you going to be doing? Getting all of your uniforms ready for next week?"

"Yep." She replied quickly. "It will be strange just going to the station and not coming here."

"I know all of you are ready to get back to your regular jobs.'

Sam was there to pick me up at the end of the day. "I thought after we take care of Molly we could go eat at the Green Sombrero. I'm in the mood for Mexican food and we should celebrate." He suggested.

"What are we celebrating?"

"The end of the month. We haven't heard from Mr. X in two weeks and you are still alive and kicking." He answered with a big smile.

"Sounds like a plan to me. Let's do it!" I agreed wholeheartedly.

"Welcome back, Detective Reynolds," Mandy greeted cheerfully. "We haven't seen you in a long time! Your table is ready for you." She led the way to the corner booth we sat in the first time we came. "Did you catch that man yet?"

"No, Mandy, we haven't. We have reason to believe he's moved on to somewhere else."

"Good; as long as he's not around here!" She exclaimed. "Bobbi Sue will be with you in a minute."

"Fajitas OK with you?" Sam asked me as we slid into the booth.

"Of course!" I responded with a look that said, "Why would we want anything else?"

"I got a call from Big Mound this afternoon." Sam said with a tone of voice I couldn't quite identify.

"I don't like the way you say that." I indicated with furrowed brows. Bobbi Sue brought the green sombrero shaped bowl with chips and salsa to the table.

"Hi, Detective Reynolds! We have been missing you! Are you going to have the usual?" She asked with a big smile.

Sam nodded. "Thanks, Bobbi Sue. Yes, it will be the usual; if it hasn't been so long that you've forgotten what that is!" They both laughed and she gave him a thumbs up. He turned back to me. "The Investigator found a witness that placed the husband at the scene of the crime when he was supposed to be on the road. The neighbors were returning home from the movies about nine o'clock and they saw the husband pulling out of his driveway. When the Officer presented that information to him; the husband confessed." Sam watched me intently to gage my reaction as I stared blankly at the bowl of chips and salsa.

"There goes your theory about the flowers and the card." I determined. "They weren't there because they weren't mentioned in the newspaper. He didn't know; no one but the real killer would know that information." I surmised. Sam scooted closer and reached for my hand. "Where does that leave us...what do I do with that information?" I looked at him in confusion.

"I'm not sure. There has been no contact from him in two weeks, when prior to that it was almost every day. He did not order flowers for you. It is as if he just suddenly vanished. I don't know if he left the area, has been arrested for something else, or what!" He exclaimed with a big sigh. "I wish I had a definite answer for you. We have not made any arrests in the past two weeks but he could have been picked up anywhere. Nobody in town has died recently. We don't even know if he lived here in the first place." Sam's frustration was evident.

The fajitas arrived with their customary sizzling, smoking, delicious odor. Sam blessed our food and we ate in silence for several minutes. "Sam, I feel so uneasy about all of this." I confessed.

"I suspect you feel something like I do when I have a case that remains unsolved. There is something unsettling about not having a solution or conclusion; there is no closure." He replied in a compassionate tone. "I wish I could fix it for you."

"I guess it will just take time... to prove it's really over."

"You are probably right. Let's talk about something else," he suggested. "I want to talk about our future together not what has happened in the past. I thank God I found you." His eyes shone with love and his smile was meant for me alone. "I want to give you the world; shower you with gifts so you will know how much I love you." He spoke in a quiet intimate tone.

"Oh, Sam," I responded softly. "*You* are all I need. You do not have to give me things to prove your love for me. I can see it in your eyes and feel it when you hold me close. I can hear it in your voice."

He leaned over and kissed me with a tender passion. "I wish July fifteenth wasn't so far away." He whispered huskily.

"Oh, my!" I took a deep breath. "We're going to get in trouble if we don't stop this." I warned. "What time are you picking me up tomorrow?" I changed the subject abruptly.

"I'm sorry," he said almost inaudibly as he closed his eyes and shook his head slightly. He scooted away from me and ate a few chips before answering. "I figure we should leave about eleven. The Mayor has called a press conference in the morning at ten to officially present me as the new Chief of Police. It should not take too long and I will pick you up when that's over. It will take us about an hour, maybe a little more, to get there and they are open until eight tomorrow night. Surely, that will be enough time to make our choices; how hard can it be?" he laughed.

Sam checked his watch. "Oh, I didn't realize that we've been here so long. I guess I should take you home." He spoke with disbelief. When we arrived at the apartments Sam walked me up upstairs. We agreed it was best to say good night at the door.

Chapter 42
Saturday, April 1

Saturday morning dawned with clear skies promising a beautiful, sunny day. My heart was so full of joy I hummed as Molly and I walked down the stairs and around to the lot behind the apartments. Spring was in full bloom. The Azalea bushes were heavy with blooms ranging in color from light pinks to deep reds. The delicate purple blossoms on the Red Bud trees enhanced their beauty. Molly was frisky in the cool morning air; she ran, jumped, and played in the emerging sunbeams that were shining through the branches. I laughed as she darted after the squirrels that were running from tree to tree; teasing her with their chatter and staying just beyond her reach.

Back in the apartment, I made tuna salad for sandwiches to take with us for lunch. I had just finished putting the last one in a baggie when there was a knock at the door. I looked at the clock. Ten fifteen. "It's too soon for Sam to be here," I told Molly as I headed for the door. She barked and ran ahead of me. "Who is it?" I called through the closed door.

"Floral delivery for Janet Carter."

"He really doesn't have to keep sending me flowers," I said to Molly unlatching the safety chain. "But I do like them," I smiled as I opened the door. My smiled turned to horror as the hooded figure with the fake brown beard pushed his way into the apartment. Molly started growling. I shrunk back. "Get out!" I commanded staring at the familiar flower arrangement with the big lime green bow. "I don't want you here."

"I will…when I'm through. And it really doesn't matter *what* you want." He replied with a sneer. His voice hit me like a slap in the face; sending waves of terror through my body. He closed and locked the door behind him. "Get over there," he ordered threateningly while pointing toward the table. He put the flowers down and held out the card with the purple Irises. I refused to take it so he threw it on the table next to the flowers.

"Why are you doing this?" I demanded as I backed away from him. Molly lunged at him and grabbed the leg of his sweatpants. He kicked hard and flung her against the wall with a thud. She yelped in pain.

"Stop it! Leave her alone." I stood up to him. The eyes that looked back at me were full of disgust. "What do you want? Why are you here?" I demanded with more courage than I felt.

"I think you know the answer to that," he scoffed with disdain. We both jumped when the telephone started ringing. He grabbed Molly and held her by the neck. "Answer that; and be careful what you say or she's dead!" He hissed.

"Hello?" I spoke into the receiver as Mr. X hovered near me to be able to hear the caller's responses.

"Hi beautiful. I hate to have to tell you this but something has come up and I am going to be late. How's your day going?" Sam inquired cheerfully.

"Oh, it's OK. I just got some flowers…" Mr. X squeezed Molly's throat and she struggled in his grasp. "…from my parents. Mom wanted to wish us luck on making decisions on stuff for the house."

"Oh, that's nice." He responded distractedly. "I'm coming," he said to someone in the room with him. "Yeah… I'll meet you in the car." Returning to me, he continued, "Listen sweetheart, I'll see you in an hour or so. I love you."

"I love you too, Sam," I replied. He hung up leaving me alone with death. The silence was deafening.

"*I love you too, Sam*," Mr. X mocked in a falsetto voice. "Good job." He added as he released Molly from where he held her in midair. I winced as she hit the floor and started to cough. I reached to pick her up. "Get away from her!" he demanded through clenched teeth.

He stepped toward me. I stepped back. "Why are you doing this? Why me? Why any of us?" I prodded, all the while trying to think of some way to get away from this horrible nightmare.

"You think you're special, don't you? You *all* do!" He spat vehemently. "You think nothing of crushing the hearts of the children you teach… ridiculing them in front of everyone… Taking their innocence and stomping it into the ground," He sneered accusingly, his eyes blazing with hatred.

"What are you talking about?"

"I loved her. And she humiliated me in front of everybody. I wrote a poem for her birthday, telling her how I felt and she laughed at me in front of the whole class. Then she had the gall to tell us that she was marrying the 'man of her dreams.' Do you know how it is to be a shy, introverted boy just coming into puberty… finally getting up the nerve to tell his teacher how wonderful he thought she was… after she had spent time with him after school to help him catch up with his peers…? She just shrugged it off as if I was nothing to her. And you…" He stuck his finger in my face. "You said you weren't coming here to find a husband!"

"W-w-what?" I stammered in confusion. He reached up and removed the fake beard. I gasped in shock. "Mr. Nicholas?" I could not believe my eyes.

"I'm going to teach *you* a lesson." He grabbed for me but I was able to dodge him and jump back beyond his reach.

"Wait, at least answer one question before you do this," I begged; trying to stall for time; hoping against all hope that Sam would have understood my veiled plea for help.

"What is it?" He smirked. His voice was cold and calculating.

"Is somebody else working with you on these murders?"

"An accomplice in crime? No!" He snapped, looking insulted. "Why would I want to share this with anyone else? This pleasure is all mine."

"Then why did you stab Barbara Adams?" I inquired.

"Because she got away from me and ran to the kitchen and picked up a big knife. She tried to stab me but I managed to wrestle it away from her. That was messy. I didn't enjoy that one." He relayed the story with no sign of remorse; almost as if it was her fault that he killed her. "Now it's *your* turn." He glared at me, his eyes gleaming with maliciousness. I shivered at the wickedness and loathing that filled his voice.

"Why didn't you come after me before now?" I asked.

"I'm not stupid." He informed me sarcastically. "You were surrounded by all those cops. You *all* were. Besides, I enjoyed watching you squirm. That was very entertaining. Except for that chicken-hearted Martinez woman; she just didn't know how to have fun." His voice dripped with contempt.

"You don't have to do this. You are not thinking straight. I can get Sam to get you some help." I tried to reason with him.

"I don't need any help. I am thinking perfectly straight and I know exactly what I'm doing." His voice resonated with madness. He let out a strange laugh and I shuddered at the remembrance of that same laughter on the telephone that Friday night we waited for him.

"Police! Open the door!" Sam's voice boomed as he banged on the door.

"Sam!" I screamed.

W. Kay Lynn

Mr. Nicholas leaped at me and grabbed me around the neck. "You'll be dead before he can get to you." He sneered. His hands tightened on my throat. I could not breathe. The pressure on my neck was excruciatingly painful. I frantically struggled against him; pummeling my fists against his face and chest but he would not break his grasp. I clawed at his hands but he was stronger than I could manage. I could hear Sam battering against the door with his shoulder. Finally, as everything was going dark I heard the splintering of wood and we were immediately hit with a force that knocked us down. Mr. Nicholas fell on top of me and lost his grip on my neck. I rolled over and started coughing and gasping for air. Mr. Nicholas was jerked up and away from me.

"We'll take care of him, Chief. You check on Miss Carter." I recognized Jackson's voice. I heard scuffling and angry muttering as they forced Mr. Nicholas into submission.

Sam was immediately by my side. He gathered me into his arms, lifted me up and carried me to the bedroom. He laid me on the bed and then sat on the edge of the bed holding me tightly. He rocked me back and forth, "Janet, oh, Janet. I am so sorry. I wasn't here." His voice was full of anguish.

"M...Mol...," I tried to speak but my voice came out in a raspy squeak.

"Don't try to talk. She's OK. Chase has her." He told me. And then he said the second most beautiful words I have ever heard. "It's over, Janet. It is finally over! He can't hurt you anymore."

Chapter 43
Saturday, April 1

The Emergency Room Doctor informed me that my voice should return to normal when the bruising on my vocal chords healed. He cautioned me not to talk for the next ten to fourteen days or the damage could become permanent; which meant it would not do me any good to go to school. I figured I could cover up and hide the bruises on the outside of my neck but I would be of no use in the classroom without the ability to speak. He released me to go home to rest, to the apartment where I had almost died earlier in the day.

The maintenance man was working to repair the doorframe when we arrived back at the apartment. I noticed that the flowers and card had been removed. Sam ushered me to the bedroom with instructions to go to bed and stay there.

Linda remained with me while Sam went to the station to work on the report for this morning's occurrences and then to the jail to interrogate Mr. Nicholas. Before he left, Sam handed me a pad of paper and a pencil. "Under NO circumstances are you to use your voice. You can write down anything you need or want to say. Chase will be here to take care of Molly. You need to stay in bed and try to get some rest. Is that clear?" He instructed me in a firm authoritarian voice.

"Yes, Sir!!!" I wrote on my paper. He kissed me on the forehead as tears trickled down my cheeks. I did not want him to go.

After he left, I fell into a fitful sleep. Linda woke me. "Are you having bad dreams?" she asked with concern. "You are making some awful noises. That can't be good for you." She looked thoughtful for a few minutes and then said, "I'll be right back." I could hear her talking on the phone. About eight minutes later, she came back with a cup of tomato soup. "Reynolds said to keep you awake until he gets back. I thought something warm might feel good to your throat." She sat on the end of the bed.

I smiled and nodded. Molly limped into the bedroom with her tail tucked between her legs. I patted the bed; her ears perked up and she gave a little tail wag. She put her front paws on the bed but she would not, or could not, jump up. I reached down and lifted her up. She started licking my chin. Tears welled up in my eyes and spilled down my cheeks. I looked at Linda with concern.

"I think she's probably sore. She should be OK in a few days. You've both been through a really harsh experience." She noted sympathetically. "You want to play cards or something?" I shook my head. You want me to stop pestering you?" She smiled. I smiled back, shook my head again and took a sip of soup. It hurt to swallow.

A short time later Sam showed up with a box of instant potatoes, a couple of cans of soup, several flavors of Jell-O, two cans of dog food, and some magazines he picked up at the store. Linda took the food items to the kitchen; Sam sat down on the side of the bed and handed me the stack of magazines; the latest copies of Woman's Day, Family Circle, and Bride's. I looked up at him; my mouth opened in surprise and delight. "Don't you say anything!" He warned holding up his right index finger. "Chase suggested the bride book. I figured you, *and* Molly, needed some soft things to eat."

"You're very thoughtful. Thanks," I wrote on my note pad. I gave him a big smile when I showed him the paper.

Linda returned from the kitchen carrying a tray of hot chocolate. "Thought we could all use a little comfort drink." Sam handed me a cup and took one for himself. Linda sat on the opposite side of the bed from Sam.

"Do you want to hear what I learned from my interview with Nicholas?" He asked gently. "Or is it too soon?" He added understandingly.

I shook my head and motioned for him to continue. Then I grabbed my tablet and wrote, "You're looking for closure?"

He smiled and nodded. "For all of us." He said quietly taking my hand and giving it a gentle squeeze.

"George Nicholas is a man with a lot of issues and deep seated anger that I never suspected." He began. "From what I gather, he didn't have a very supportive mother-figure in his life. She had a lot of emotional problems; in and out of mental institutions. When she *was* at home, she did not have much to do with him.

"He failed the sixth grade and ended up having the same teacher again the next year. She, apparently, took pity on him and tutored him after school most of that second year trying to help him catch up with the rest of the class. For her birthday, which must have been toward the end of the year, the class got together and threw a big party for her. Different kids did different presentations…skits, songs, what have you. Nicholas wrote a poem expressing his feelings for her and when she told him it was sweet but she had a boyfriend; he took that as a personal rejection. The other kids in class laughed at him and teased him about it. Later in the party, the fiancé showed up and that was like rubbing salt in his wounds.

"Zoom up to last November; the week before Thanksgiving. His wife told him she wanted a divorce; she had met someone else." Sam paused and waited until I gave him a nod and indicated for him to continue. "She was a teacher when they first married. She stopped teaching when they had their first child. On a hunch, I checked it out… she left him two days after the new moon. That was apparently his breaking point. He snapped and we know what happened after that."

I closed my eyes and shuddered. Sam moved to the head of the bed to sit beside me. I scooted over so I could lean back against him. He put his arms around me and continued to recount the story. I shook my head; I picked up my tablet. "No more for now, please. I am tired. I can't listen to any more. You can finish later. I'm sorry."

"It's OK, sweetheart. I know this is hard. Do you think you could sleep?" He asked quietly before placing a kiss on my temple. I shrugged my shoulders.

"I'll tell you what," Linda offered. "I'll take Molly outside for a little while so you two can have some quiet time. Get some rest." She patted my foot then she picked up Molly and left the room. A minute later I heard her go out the front door.

I scribbled on the note pad, "Will you sing for me?"

"Of course, I will. Any special request?" I shook my head and he started singing. His beautiful voice soothed my jangled nerves and enveloped me with God's peace and love.

"I come to the garden alone
While the dew is still on the roses
And the voice I hear falling on my ear
The Son of God discloses.

And He walks with me, and He talks with me,
And He tells me I am His own;
And the joy we share as we tarry there,
None other has ever known.

He speaks, and the sound of His voice,

W. Kay Lynn

Is so sweet the birds hush their singing,
And the melody that He gave to me
Within my heart is ringing.

And He walks with me, and He talks with me,
And He tells me I am His own;
And the joy we share as we tarry there,
None other has ever known.

I'd stay in the garden with Him
Though the night around me be falling,
But He bids me go; through the voice of woe
His voice to me is calling.

And He walks with me, and He talks with me,
And He tells me I am His own;
And the joy we share as we tarry there,
None other has ever known."[7]

The tension slowly left my body; fading as the comforting sounds of his voice reassured me. I relaxed and snuggled back in his arms; I was safe. I fell asleep before he finished the last refrain. Sometime later, I opened my eyes to see Linda sitting in a chair she carried in from the dining table. The lamp on the bedside table cast a soft glow on the magazine she was reading.

"Hi," she whispered quietly. "How are you feeling?"

I smiled and nodded. I could tell that Sam was sleeping by the rhythm of his breathing. "What time is it?" I mouthed to her pointing at my wrist.

"Eight twenty," she answered in a hushed voice. "Are you hungry? Can I fix you some soup?"

I nodded and she headed to the kitchen. "You can bring me some, too." Sam roused and called out.

"Sorry. Didn't mean to wake you up." I wrote on the paper.

It's OK," he smiled and gave me a squeeze before dislodging himself from behind me and standing up to stretch. Sam protested when I tried to get up. "You need to stay right where you are. I drooped my shoulders and gave him a pouty, puppy dog look. "OK," he relented. "But just for a little while."

---

7 "In The Garden", Charles A. Miles, Public Domain

The Birthday Killer

Sam followed me into the living room. Suddenly, I was accosted by the repulsive vision of Mr. Nicholas attacking me; feeling his hands constricting around my neck. I whirled around and thrust myself into Sam's protective arms. He held me tightly not saying anything for a few minutes. I started to cry. "This is harder than you thought it would be, isn't it?" He said quietly. I nodded. "Do you want to go back to bed?" I shook my head. I turned slowly and walked resolutely to the table; he followed with his hands on my shoulders.

Linda placed steaming bowls of chicken noodle soup on the table and a big bowl of crackers in the middle. As soon as Sam finished saying grace, Linda spoke up. "I just want to ask a question. I know you and Jackson were headed out to the robbery-in-progress at Mayfield's Department Store this morning. How did you know to come here? What tipped you off?" She inquired.

"The grace of God," he stated matter-of-factly. Linda gave him a look of total confusion. "When the call came in", he continued. "Jackson and I were scrambling to get to Mayfield's. I wanted to let Janet know I would be late, so, I gave her a quick call. We were almost to Mayfield's when it hit me. 'Her parents are dead!' I yelled at Jackson. 'Get to Janet's now!' That's when I radioed dispatch and told them to tell you to get over here and Beckett informed me that Lakin Florist had just called in to let us know that '*that man*' had picked up flowers again. If I had not taken the time to call Janet… we would already have been at Mayfield's and out of the car. We wouldn't have heard Beckett trying to raise us on the radio." he grimaced. He reached over and took my hand. "If I hadn't gotten here in time I would have never forgiven myself." I lifted his hand to my cheek and smiled.

"How did you know it was Nicholas?" she questioned.

"I didn't… until I got here."

"How in the world did the witnesses get his description so wrong? He's shorter and thinner than what they described." She wondered.

"That's an easy one." Sam explained. "He had built up shoes which added about three inches to his height and his sweat suit was padded; adding bulk and the appearance of more weight."

Sam looked at me with concern. "You're worn out; you need to get back in the bed," he observed. I nodded slowly and let out a big sigh. I stood up and he hugged me to him. "You've got to get better fast; we've got a house to build and a wedding to plan."

39364429R00104

Made in the USA
Lexington, KY
19 February 2015